UNFORESEEN

Book Two in the Inheritance Series

By
Victoria Lynn Deviney

Copyright © 2018 by Victoria Lynn Deviney

UNFORESEEN
Book Two in the Inheritance Series

Cover picture created by Miss Mae.

Printed in the United States of America

ISBN-13: 978-1719214513
ISBN-10: 1719214514

Scripture, unless otherwise noted, taken from the HOLY BIBLE, NEW INTERNATIONAL VERSION®. Copyright © 1973, 1978, 1984 International Bible Society. Used by permission of Zondervan. All rights reserved.

All Rights Reserved. No part of this publication may be reproduced, stored in a retrieval system, or transmitted, in any form or in any means– by electronic, mechanical, photocopying, recording or otherwise– without prior written permission.

To purchase additional copies of this book, visit amazon.com.

DEDICATION

TO MY WONDERFUL HUSBAND DAN.
THANK YOU FOR BELIEVING IN
ME AND FOR ALLOWING ME
TO DO WHAT I LOVE THE MOST!

FOREWORD

To know Victoria Deviney, is to know a woman of character, integrity, Christlikeness, and prayer. These godly characteristics, however, don't for a minute lessen her infectious personality and great sense of humor. As much as Victoria is someone you would seek out for godly counsel, she is a natural at bringing a crowd alive with her great stories, shared with a laughter that frees those around her to be comfortable with themselves. It's out of this unique gifting of the Lord that Victoria writes with such creativity and depth.

In "A Moment's Notice", Victoria developed a community of characters that were real and engaging and a plot that kept me guessing to the very end, and beyond. This sequel is a "must" as the previous story continues and a new one unfolds.

J. Michael Chalmers, Counsellor
Courageous Counselling Ministry, Greenville, South Carolina.

Unforeseen, Book two in the Inheritance Series, Group Members

Martha	Paralegal who works for lawyer/boyfriend, Stuart
Trent	Youth pastor, married to Maggie
Henry	Retired businessman
Terry	Realtor engaged to Jeffrey
Claire	Secretary to Mr. Peterson

A Moment's Notice, Book One in the Inheritance Series, Group Members

Nicole	Home-maker, cancer patient, married to Rob. (After Katy died, Nicole took over the shelters for abused women.)
Katy	Stay-at-home mother, opened up shelters for abused women, married to Tom (Henry's son)
Clay	Investment broker
Matthew	Became a missionary in Sudan after the challenge, married to Melissa
Claire	Secretary to Mr. Peterson

INTRODUCTION

Many search for peace, joy, and contentment in material things. Yet they find it elusive in any other avenue except in the person of Jesus Christ.

What starts out as a monetary inheritance given to four individuals soon leads to challenges, twists and turns, that they are all unprepared for.

Walking into an "Unforeseen" future—broken, afraid, hurt and searching—they learn more about themselves and each other than they realize. As a result, each will walk out with a newfound faith, courage, and a transformed life that only comes from meeting God face to face.

Victoria Lynn Deviney

Chapter 1

Terry walked out of her upscale condo and onto the sidewalk below. Looking up she admired the glass and architecture of her city. She loved being in the midst of all the hustle and bustle. It made her smile. Just then her phone buzzed. She grabbed it quickly, scanned the number, but didn't recognize it. Deciding to answer just in case it was a client, she said, "Hello," in her most businesslike voice.

"Ms. Morgan?" said the lady on the other line.

"Yes, how can I help you?"

"My name is Claire, and it is my pleasure to inform you that you have acquired a sum of money from a Mr. Peterson, and we are to read the will in just a few days. Would you be available to attend a brief meeting?"

"Why, I'm not sure. I really don't know a Mr. Peterson, and I'm a little surprised that I would be receiving money from someone I'm not familiar with."

"I feel that most of your questions will be answered once you're here. The meeting will be on Thursday at 9:15am, on the fifteenth floor of the Anderson building."

"Oh, I know where the building is located, but I will have to check my calendar once I am at work, and let you know after that."

"Very well," Claire responded. "We hope to hear from you soon. Have a good day."

Terry laughed to herself, flagging down the first taxi she saw. *What a call to get first thing in the morning,* she thought.

Henry sat on the bench at the park, feeding the geese, when something began to vibrate in his shirt pocket. It took him a minute to realize what was happening. Chuckling to himself, he realized that he kept forgetting he had a phone now—thanks to his children, who thought he needed a way to communicate with them. As he clicked on the green button, he heard a woman's voice saying, "Hello."

"Yes, hello," he said slowly.

"Is this Mr. Henry Jamison?"

"Yes, Yes, it is. How can I help you, Miss?"

"My name is Claire, and I am calling to let you know of an inheritance you have received."

"Really, who would be giving me that?" he grinned.

"Mr. Peterson," Claire stated, "and if you could spare a little of your time, we are meeting on Thursday morning at 9:15 on the fifteenth floor of the Anderson building, downtown."

Henry sat stunned for a minute and couldn't speak.

"Mr. Jamison are you still there?"

"Uh, yes. I'm sorry what did you say this man's name was, Mr. Peterson? I don't think I'll be able to come to the meeting, but I do thank you for calling and letting me know about it. And

I really don't drive into the city anymore, but I tell you what I'll do. I'll pray about it and if you see me there then you'll know my answer, how's that?"

"Well, I guess that will be fine," Claire responded with a slight laugh.

"Well, OK, Miss Claire. You have a good day now."

"You too, Mr. Jamison. It was a pleasure talking to you."

Sitting down at her desk, Martha savored her first cup of coffee at the beginning of the day. She looked at her calendar when her phone rang loudly. Looking around to see if anyone else might answer, she sighed and picked it up. "Houghton, Houghton and Melton," she said, almost without thought.

"Yes, may I speak to Mrs. Martha Turner?"

"This is she. How can I help you?"

"Mrs. Turner, my name is Claire, and I am calling to inform you of an inheritance that you have been given."

"What?" Martha said almost too loudly!

"Yes, your presence is requested on Thursday at 9:15am on the fifteenth floor of the Anderson building."

"I'm sorry, who did you say you were?"

"Claire, and I am calling on behalf of Mr. Peterson."

"I don't believe I know a Mr. Peterson. Is he a client of ours?"

"No, he is deceased, and the one from whom you are getting an inheritance."

"Really, I don't understand," Martha said exasperated.

"That's not important," Claire insisted, "but what is important, is that you attend the up-coming meeting on Thursday morning."

"Well, I cannot commit to it, but I will check and see."

"Thank you," Claire said, "and we hope you'll make the right decision to come."

"Well, whether I come or not will be for me to decide," she stated curtly.

"Very well," Claire replied.

Trent carried his toddler out to the car and buckled him up for the drive to the daycare center.

"Honey," his wife yelled from the house, "do you have his blanket?"

"Yes, I grabbed it on the way out the door."

"Great," she said as she turned back to lock the door. Then, looking in her purse, she noticed she had forgotten her cell phone. "Shoot," she mumbled, "I must have left it on the kitchen counter."

Running to the car, she jumped in. Frazzled, she smiled as Trent gave her that knowing look. Driving the half hour to the church gave both a chance to spend a little more time with each other.

"It seems we are always working." He looked over at her and noticed she was emailing a note to her boss.

"I know," she said, looking up. "We really need to have a scheduled date night each week and make it a priority."

"Yes, we do. So how about Thursday evening at our favorite restaurant?"

"Sounds good to me," she leaned over to kiss his cheek. As she looked back at their son Jacob, she noticed, as she had so many times before, how much he looked like his father.

Suddenly Trent's phone rang that familiar song they both loved. Reaching down he pressed the speaker and said, "Hello."

"Yes, hello," Claire responded, "is this Trent Bowers?"

"Why yes, it is. How can I help you?"

"Well, it is my hope that I can help you."

"OK," he smiled, as he glanced over at Maggie busily working on her iPad.

"You are invited to a meeting on Thursday morning at 9:15 at the Anderson building."

Interrupting, Trent asked, "Is this work related?"

"No, it's about an inheritance that a Mr. Peterson has left you."

"Um, I don't seem to recall knowing this gentleman," he said.

"Well, I am sure it will be clear very soon. The meeting is on the fifteenth floor. We hope to see you there."

"OK, thanks for the information. If I have any other questions, is this a good number to get back to you?"

"Yes, this is my cell. Feel free to call anytime, and I hope you have a good day, Mr. Drew."

"Good day to you too," he said as he slipped the phone back into his pocket. "We'll that was strange," he commented.

"Who was it?" Maggie asked as she looked up from her iPad.

"A woman named Claire, saying that a Mr. Peterson had left me an inheritance. For the life of me I cannot think of where I've met this man."

"Well, who cares? We may get some needed money to pay off some bills, and for that I will be grateful."

Chapter 2

Terry woke up suddenly, throwing off her covers. Feeling a vague sense of doom, she looked over to see that it was only 5:30am. Lying back down, she thought about how she had been plagued with the same nightmare for over twenty years—she felt as if she were suffocating right before waking. Staring at the ceiling, she then remembered that strange phone call she'd received just a few days ago about some kind of inheritance.

Turning over to get up, the phone rang, and she heard Jeffery's voice on the other end.

"Hey Beautiful."

"Hey yourself," she smiled. "What are you doing calling me so early?"

"Well, I just thought you might want to get an early start today seeing that it's my birthday!"

"Is it?" she said coyly.

"You know it is," Jeffery shot back playfully. "So how about having a cup of coffee with your fiancé?"

"Well, I guess I can spare an hour before work," she said laughing.

"Great, I will see you in an hour then."

"In that case, I better jump in the shower and get ready," she said, hanging up mid-sentence.

Jeffery rang the doorbell promptly at 7:30am. Terry grinned seeing him as he stood there with two lattes and a bag of bagels.

"You're always right on time, aren't you?"

"Of course, that and my suave looks stole your heart, remember?" He grinned as she reached up to kiss him on the cheek. He took her in his arms and gave her a nice long kiss. "Um," she touched his face, "that's always a good way to start off the day!"

Handing her a cup of coffee, he led her out to the terrace that was already warmed by the sun. "This is long overdue," he sighed, looking towards the city.

She looked into his eyes and said, "My job has me working all the time, and we haven't had a date in a while, have we? But my commission from selling homes and my bonuses will certainly help offset some of our wedding costs."

"I know, I know," Jeffery said smiling. "I just miss you, that's all." Grabbing her hand, he pulled her towards him. She felt that deep longing of needing to be loved that she always seemed to crave, yet never got enough of.

Henry Jamison was walking down the sidewalk when little Stella came running up to him carrying her baby doll. "So, what brings you out so early this morning?" he asked, grinning at the toothless little girl.

"The tooth fairy came to see me last night," she said, as her arm shot out to show him the crisp five-dollar bill in her little hand.

"Wow! The tooth fairy certainly gives better gifts these days," he chuckled.

"I'm going with my mom to the store after she gets off work this afternoon, and I'm buying some shoes for my doll."

"That's nice," Henry said, as he stooped down to get his newspaper, which was partially hidden under the shrubbery. "Oh, my aching back," he said as he grabbed hold of the bush. "I wish these boys would learn how to throw the paper up on the porch."

"You want me to get it for you?" Stella said as she sat her doll down "I can crawl in there easier."

"Would you?" Henry asked? "Be careful though, wouldn't want anything to get you."

"I'm not afraid," Stella said as she handed him the paper. "I do this all the time for my dad too."

"Really?" Henry said. Stella looked up at his bright blue eyes and motioned him to bend down towards her. She grabbed his face with her little hands, pulled him towards her, and kissed him right on the mouth before he could do anything! Startled he laughed, "What was that for young lady?"

"Oh, I just wanted to," she laughed, and turned to leave. "Gotta go. My mom will wonder where I am so early!"

"See you soon," he waved, watching her trot off across the street. Watching her skip down the sidewalk he said, "Such a cute little girl." *Reminds me of my Marisa so very long ago,* he thought. *Lord, I sure do miss her. I would love to see her again before I get much older. It's been over ten years since I have seen her face.*

As he turned to go back inside, he looked up and noticed that little Stella had stopped and was waving back to him. He lifted up his hand and smiled. Just then that familiar beep went off in the top of his shirt pocket. He looked and saw that it was a reminder message about a meeting downtown.

Trent finished his sandwich quickly wiping the crumbs off his shirt, just as the Senior Pastor came strolling in. Getting up to shake his hand, he noticed that a big piece of cheese had rolled onto the floor. "Sorry, Pastor, you caught me taking a quick lunch break. I'm running a little behind today."

"That's OK, keep your seat," the tall man said grinning. "Just came by to see if you could work some overtime this weekend?"

"Sure," Trent said, "that is if I can leave on Friday by 4:30. It's my wife's birthday, and I've made some plans."

"Of course, the Pastor nodded. "We don't want our wives unhappy, now do we?"

Grinning, mostly to himself, he nodded, No. Then he glanced down at his calendar and noticed he had a meeting tomorrow morning at the Anderson building. "I also have a meeting downtown at 9:00am on Thursday. Hope that's going to be OK with your schedule?"

"That's fine. I just need someone to be here all day on Friday. I'm going to be tied up at a Ministers' meeting."

"Great, I would be glad to."

"Thanks," the Pastor said as he headed out the door.

Martha walked into her house, throwing her coat and pocketbook on the chair. As she sat down on the couch, she thought about the odd phone call that morning. Closing her eyes, she secretly wished the inheritance would be a cool million dollars. She would take off for a nice long vacation out of the country, away from everyone. Grinning she knew that was only a pipe dream.

Unforeseen

What was the name of that lady, she thought, *Claire, that was it.* She sat there thinking, *perhaps I should give her a call tonight and let her know that I've had a hard week and won't be able to make it. Or maybe, just maybe this is the universe's way of getting me out of my routine, this boring job. One never knows, does one?*

Then she found herself drifting off, and dreaming of long white beaches, and sand as soft as the plush carpet underneath her feet.

Chapter 3

Before the first person showed up, Claire had gathered up all the information. At 9:15am, she wondered if anyone would come, and then the door opened, and Trent strolled in. "Am I late?" he asked, as he came over to shake her hand.

"Yes, you are," Claire said ginning, "but that's OK. "Feel free to grab a snack and a cup of coffee. We still have three more that are supposed to come."

"Really? I didn't know this was a shared inheritance?"

"Yes, there are a few surprises that you'll be finding out soon enough."

"Well, I hope this isn't some scam where we give you our credit card in hopes of winning some sort of lottery."

"No, no. It's not a surprise like that, I can assure you." Claire smiled.

As Trent sat down to eat, he looked out the massive window that faced towards the city. "Wow, what a view. I bet you don't get tired of seeing that every day?"

Claire looked up towards the glimmering skyline, "I guess I need to look more often. I tend to get busy and forget I'm even up here. Thanks for the reminder. Well, feel free to enjoy the view, I'm hoping the others will be here in a few minutes," she said as she headed back to her office.

Trent leaned back in his chair wondering about the inheritance, "Well, maybe if I'm the only one who shows up, they'll give me the whole enchilada," he said, half laughing to himself!

♦ ♦ ♦

Terry looked down at her watch as she headed towards the stairs of her office building. Tall and lanky, she ran everywhere she went. *Well, at least the building is just around the corner, so I can walk instead of flagging down a taxi*, she thought. Coming into the lobby of the Anderson building, she noticed a well-dressed older lady standing there, waiting for the elevator. As the door opened, both stepped into the elevator and pushed the same button for the 15th floor.

Martha, who seemed to be in her own little world, looked up and suddenly noticed the dark-headed woman with bright blue eyes. "Looks like we're headed to the same floor," she said.

"Why yes, it does, as a matter of fact," Terry replied.

"That's a little strange," Martha frowned.

"Really?" Terry said.

Martha continued, "Well, are you here for the inheritance meeting too?"

"Yes, I sure am," Terry said smiling.

"Well, I hope we're not wasting our time on some sort of scam," Martha said briskly.

Victoria Lynn Deviney

For some reason Henry woke up early that morning. Sipping his coffee and reading his Bible, he suddenly heard that familiar beeping. He began picking up pillows and books to see where his phone might be. Finally, he found it tucked inside the pocket of the old shirt pocket he'd worn the day before. Quickly opening it, he noticed a message alerting him of the inheritance meeting this morning.

Claire was at her desk wondering if she needed to reschedule the meeting when she heard the elevator door open. Standing up, she walked out into the hallway and noticed two very attractive women looking around. "Well, hello there, you must be Terry and Martha?"

"Yes, that would be us," Martha spoke up.

"Is this where the meeting is supposed to be?" Terry added.

"Yes, it is," Claire smiled. "Please come with me. We are waiting for one more, but feel free to have a snack and cup of coffee!" Just then her phone vibrated in her pocket. "Excuse me," she said and walked back out into the hallway. "Hello?"

"This is Henry Jamison, is this Claire?"

"Yes, Henry. We're waiting for you, are you coming? Everyone else is here already."

"I understand, but I just remembered the meeting, and I'm still at home. You may want to go ahead and start without me."

"But we really need you to be here, Mr. Jamison. If I send a car over to pick you up, do you think you could be ready?"

"You just don't give up, do you?" Henry remarked.

"I guess I don't," Claire laughed.

"Well," Henry sighed and said slowly, "what can it hurt? But I don't want to be any trouble."

"Don't worry about it. Just let me write your address down, and someone will be there in ten minutes."

"Well, OK. Tell him I will be waiting outside on my front porch swing."

"Great! I will let everyone know you're on your way then." Turning around to see the women and Trent talking, Claire headed towards the room.

Chapter 4

The limo swung around the cul-de-sac several times before noticing the modest home where the old man sat waiting. "Hi there," the driver waved as he got out.

"Good morning," Henry answered, with a twinkle in his eye. "So, you're the one picking me up for this mysterious meeting?"

"Sure am," the young guy said, as he extended his hand towards Henry. "So, are you ready to go? We're running a little late, and Claire told me to make it quick!"

"Sure, let me just get my keys and lock the door." As the old man got in the car, he noticed his neighbors all looking out their windows. Chuckling, he said to the driver, "Let me tell you that I will be the talk around the dinner table tonight!"

Laughing, the young man turned to him and added, "You're probably right. They're all going to want to know the scoop about the limo, for sure."

They continued to talk until they arrived downtown. Suddenly the old man got very quiet, and the driver looked in his rearview mirror to see if he was okay. "Looks like you're deep in thought?"

"Yes, it's been a long time since I've been downtown, especially to the Anderson building."

"What kind of work did you do, if I may ask, Sir?"

"Oh, I was an architect and somewhat of a philanthropist."

"Wow! So, did you buy buildings and restore them back to the original condition?"

"Sure did. Even the one you're dropping me off at today."

"Well, that's something else," the young man said smiling. "May I ask you another personal question?"

"Sure, anything," the old man grinned. "I'm an open book nowadays."

"Was the Anderson building named after you?"

The old man paused as if pondering the question, "Why would you ask me this, Son?"

"Well, isn't your last name Anderson, Sir?"

"Yes, but I haven't gone by that name in a while. I use my middle name Jamison. So how it is that you know this information?"

"Well, Claire told me your full name, but that you went by Jamison for some reason."

Henry sat there staring out the window for a long time. "Guess you can't keep your identity a secret forever, can you?"

"Well, not that it's any of my business. But why would you want to? I mean you must be a pretty important man, if I may say so?"

"Well, I don't look at myself that way now. But unfortunately, I guess I was at one time. Back then I would have done anything for prestige and money. I know I don't look the part," the old man gestured with his hand, "but I was a workaholic, and business was my life, which excluded my immediate family, I'm sorry to say."

The young man was silent for a moment. "My dad was a lot like you, all work and no play. Hardly ever saw him, but I came out okay."

"Yes, it seems you did," the old man smiled. "Mine was a different story. I lost what I had very quickly—my family that is. My wife left with the children, and the sad thing about that was, I was too busy to even notice their departure. I tried to call and get them to come back home. Guess I thought I could buy their love as easily as I bought buildings. But I quickly realized that true love can't be bought or sold."

"Um, that's deep," the young man said thoughtfully. "I appreciate your honesty in telling me this. Guess it still hurts a lot?"

"Yes, my ex-wife died a few years ago. She had married again, and we did get things straightened out before she passed, but my children are another thing. My daughter even bought me a phone not long ago, so we could keep in touch more. But that hasn't made that much of a difference. Anyway, without the Lord's forgiveness ... ", and his voice drifted off.

Suddenly the car stopped, and Henry realized they were at the destination. "Well, it's been a pleasure talking to you," Henry gestured, "and thanks again for coming to pick me up!"

"You're very welcome, Mr. Anderson—I mean, Mr. Jamison. The pleasure was all mine!"

"That's OK, Son. Don't worry about it. I'm not sure why I've tried to hide my name. Guess I just didn't want a lot of questions, you know. Brings back too many hurtful memories!"

"I understand. Even at my age, I've done some things I'm not proud of either. Can I pick you up when your meeting is over?"

"No, thank you," Henry replied. "I think I'll grab a bite to eat around here before I go home."

"Well, how will you get back?" the young man asked.

"Why, the bus of course! I'm not too good to ride it once in a while," he grinned.

Unforeseen

"No, I guess not," the young man smiled.

As the old man headed into the building, he turned back and smiled. The young man waved back, for he knew in his heart that the Lord had spoken to him through Henry that morning.

Chapter 5

Claire walked into the room and noticed the women impatiently waiting for the meeting to begin. "So sorry for the delay. Mr. Jamison just arrived, so we will be starting shortly! Please have another cup of coffee."

"I don't want another cup of coffee," Martha said gruffly. "What I want is to get my money and be on my way! It's Monday, so we all know what that means."

"Yes, I sure do," Terry chimed in. "I have two houses to close on today as well."

The only one not speaking was Trent, who was so engrossed in his emails that he paid little attention to the women.

"I understand," Claire said, "but it's very important to have everyone together, especially for the first meeting, so we don't need to repeat things twice."

Just then, Henry came walking into the room. "Well hello everyone!" the old man said smiling.

They looked up at him as if he had just landed on earth from another planet. As he looked around the room, he noticed that Terry

Unforeseen

looked a lot like his long-lost daughter, and he decided to sit next to her. She looked at him and scooted over uncomfortably.

"Now that everyone is here," Claire interrupted, "I will send in Mr. Roberts to brief you on all the specifics."

With that, a tall slender man walked in, opened his briefcase, and handed each of them an envelope. Please do not to open this until after the meeting," he instructed them.

"I am the late Mr. Peterson's lawyer, and each of you have been given a portion of his estate. What you aren't aware of is that at some point in your life, you met this man, and apparently left an impact on him. That is why you were invited here today."

Trent was the first to speak up, "If I may ask, will the contents of the envelope shed some light on this mystery?"

Mr. Roberts hesitated, "I'm really not sure what the contents of each envelope hold, but I am sure it will help answer most of your questions. I believe Claire informed you that this will be the first of several meetings you will be having."

Just then Martha interrupted him, "I don't know about everyone else, but this is ridiculous! In fact, I may just leave right now, and forget the whole thing!"

"Well, that's your choice," Mr. Roberts responded, not even missing a beat, "but let me remind you that if you do decide to opt out, then your inheritance will be divided between the other three that are here. And you just might miss a blessing that not a lot of people get a chance to experience."

With that, Martha looked around the room, and sat down quietly.

"Anyway, as I was saying, please check your calendars and see what the best day for all of you would be to meet again. There are five more meetings to attend. Then let Claire know, so she can send out a reminder each week." With that he closed his brief case and answered a few more questions. "Oh, one more thing," he said as he reached the door, I will be back once more on the fifth week, so make note of this on your calendars."

Claire came back in. Looking around at the faces, she cleared her throat. "So," she paused, "we need to see which day suits everyone for the next five weeks?"

"What exactly is the commitment?" Trent asked.

"When you read the information in your individual envelopes, you will see why it's not a cut and dry inheritance."

Henry spoke up, "Well, it will be a little difficult to come for that amount of time. I don't drive anymore, and I can't expect a limo driver to always be available to pick me up." With that everyone chuckled.

Terry scanned her schedule. "It looks like Tuesday might work for me."

"That's not good for me," Martha responded. "I have to be in court every Tuesday morning."

"OK," Trent chimed in. "How about Thursday then?"

When there was no immediate response, Henry spoke up and said, "I guess we will take this as a 'yes' from the group?"

"Guess so," everyone responded.

"Good," Claire said. "So, I will see you all here the same time next Thursday!" Everyone looked around at each other, and agreed, though not happily.

As Claire closed the door on the conference room, she had a vague feeling that this might not be as positive of an outcome as the last group had been.

Chapter 6

Martha quickly left the meeting and grabbed a taxi to her office, wondering why she'd let herself be dragged into this drama. Perhaps it was the lure of money, and the thought of a nice vacation. She'd always dreamed of going to Italy and seeing all the vineyards, and of course, tasting all the various kinds of wine. That reminded her of needing a glass just about now!

The taxi driver shouted to her the address, which made her come back to reality. Quickly grabbing her purse, she paid him, and jumped out, already dreading her busy workday.

Opening the door to the massive building, she caught herself thinking about her life. Deep down she always felt there had to be someone or something greater that created everything. But not being religious, she didn't want to even go there. Stepping into her office she reached for the ringing phone and said the familiar "Houghton and Melton" greeting. She quickly forgot about the early morning meeting.

Victoria Lynn Deviney

Trent ran to his car parked half a block down from the Anderson building. Looking back, he noticed the old man standing on the curb waiting. His mind went to all that he had to do, but he also knew that he needed to ask the man if he wanted a ride home.

"Sir," he said, Henry looked up and saw the lanky young man strolling toward him. "Do you need a ride home?"

"Well, I was thinking about grabbing a quick bite of lunch. Would you like to have lunch with an old man? I'm buying," he grinned.

"Sure, why not," Trent smiled, "where do you want to go?"

"I seem to remember a diner that was around the corner. Why don't we stroll down and see if it's still there? Used to be quite good."

As they began talking, Trent noted how quick-witted the old man was. Soon he was laughing and quickly forgot just how stressed he was. Finding the diner just where Henry thought it was, they were ushered to an old booth towards the back. "So, tell me about yourself," Henry said, as he stirred cream into his coffee.

"Not much to tell, except I have a beautiful wife, and an equally beautiful little baby boy," Trent grinned proudly.

"Why isn't that nice," Henry smiled. "So young and fresh—makes me envy you a bit, I must say!"

"Oh, I'm sure you have a nice big family too," Trent replied and smiled as he sipped his tea.

"Well, I did at one time, but that's a long story. So, what is your profession young man?"

"I work at a church not too far from here. In fact, if you would like me to pick you up next week for the meeting, I would be glad to."

"That's very kind of you," Henry looked deep into his eyes. "It's right what they say, isn't it?"

"What?" Trent said.

"That the eyes are the windows of the soul," Henry replied.

"Well, I guess," embarrassed, Trent looked down a little.

"I'm a Christian too," Henry replied. "you could say I'm a new believer—only came to faith about ten years ago."

"Really? Tell me your story," Trent said as he leaned in. And as they began to share, neither one noticed that the waitress had come with their food and gone.

Henry wiped his mouth and let out a big burp. "Oh my, I'm sorry," he said looking over at Trent. "I haven't enjoyed a hamburger and onion rings like that in quite some time!"

"No problem," Trent grinned. "I do it all the time when I'm at home, which really annoys my wife!"

The waitress asked if they wanted anything else, then left the check on the table, which Henry quickly grabbed. "I really appreciate you taking your time and having lunch with me!"

"It was my pleasure, really," Trent smiled as they both stood up to leave. "Wow, looks like we are the last people here," Trent said as he looked around and noticed most everyone had already gone.

Looking down at his old pocket watch, Henry noticed they had been talking over two hours. "I hope I haven't kept you too long!"

"No, not at all. Please let me drop you off at your house on my way to work."

"Thank you for the offer, but I think I'll take the bus home today—do something a little different."

"Are you sure? It's no problem," Trent replied.

"I appreciate it, but it will be good to take my time going home, especially since all my neighbors saw me being picked up by a limo this morning!"

As Trent walked out, he looked back and noticed the old man talking to the young waitress who'd served them and saw both laughing. Somehow, he too felt a little more refreshed and ready to tackle the day. He silently thanked the Lord for not letting him miss out on that unexpected blessing.

Terry walked into her office to find a couple already waiting on her. "So sorry," she said. "I had an early morning meeting that got started late and lasted way too long!"

"That's OK," the couple replied, "we just helped ourselves to a cup of your good coffee and a pastry!"

"I'm so glad you did! Would you like anything else?"

"Just a house!" they both said, laughing.

Smiling, Terry nodded and said, "Of course. Now let's go over those you've already made a note on!"

Thinking about the meeting, she hoped this so-called inheritance would free her from having to work so many hours. *One could only hope*, she thought.

Trent walked into church and noticed how quiet it was. Most of the staff took off on Mondays. Looking at his calendar, he knew it was going to be one busy week. *Lord, there has to be more to ministry than meetings and programs.* He had heard back in seminary that ministry burn-out was common in the staff, and he didn't want to become a statistic. *Wouldn't it be great if I could get*

away somewhere secluded, just to be by myself? Then maybe I could be a better husband, father, and minister, he thought.

"Please help me," he said silently. As he shut his door, he heard someone come into the building.

Henry sat down on the porch thinking about the morning, and about Mr. Peterson. He remembered how he had treated him long ago, and it made him feel more uncomfortable taking the inheritance money. He wondered why of all people he would be given a portion of it, especially after he had bought his building right out from underneath him? Peterson had loved that old building, and he'd begged Henry to look at other properties he had owned—but to no avail. When Henry wanted something, he always made a way to get it—regardless. Thinking about the past made Henry shiver, and he grabbed his old sweater and pulled it close around him.

Henry was used to this guilt and regret that seemed to envelope him. What hurt him the most was how he'd treated people for so many years. He had heard about Peterson's death, and just the week before felt the Lord prompting him to go and make it right. But the old embarrassment and pride had stopped him. Still deep in his thoughts, he didn't notice little Stella standing right in front of him smiling from ear to ear. Looking up, he realized that this is what he needed: some unconditional love. *Thanks God, for the reminder*, he said to himself.

Chapter 7

Trent quickly forgot about the morning meeting and the good lunch he had enjoyed with Henry as the day was full of the unexpected. Reaching for his cell phone, he called to tell his wife he would be running a little late again.

Pastor Jeff knocked lightly on his door and peeped in. "Do you have a minute?"

Trent waved him in, and quickly left a message for his wife. Anything wrong?" Trent asked as he got up to shake his hand.

"No, just wanted to speak to you a minute before I leave for my vacation."

"Sure, sit down, that is if you can find a seat," he said laughing.

"Don't worry," Pastor Jeff smiled, "you should see my office. I didn't get a chance to really clean it, but that's the way it is around here, especially in the summer! But it's a good thing, isn't it, Trent?"

"Why, yes. It is." Trent smiled.

Pastor Jeff paused, "I'm a little concerned about you. You're looking so tired lately. Is everything OK?"

Trent leaned forward and said, "Sure. Why?"

"Well, I've noticed that you've been a little distracted this past month. Although Jim is preaching for me the next two Sundays, I don't want to put undue pressure on you as well."

"No, no," Trent shook his head. "I'm fine really. Life is just a lot busier right now with the new house, and Jacob growing so fast! I'm just having to adjust to high gear, that's all."

"Well, I understand totally," said Pastor Jeff. "When I first started in the ministry, it took me a while to figure out that my wife and family came first before my church. I just don't want you to burn out when you've just begun."

"Thanks, but I'm fine, really," Trent smiled. "By the way, where are you going on your vacation, if I may ask?"

"Oh, my wife and I are going on our first cruise; she's been wanting to do this for some time now! Then we're coming back and taking the whole family to Disney World, including our grandchildren!"

"Wow, that sounds like fun!"

"Well, I hope it will be. This is the first time since I've been in ministry that I've taken three weeks off."

"Well, you deserve it." Trent grinned, secretly wishing he had time away with Marcie as well.

With that the pastor got up to leave. As he turned around he looked intently into Trent's eyes, and prayed silently that this vague sense of dread was all in his mind. "Son, if you have any problems while I'm gone, just give Jim a call, and he will try to help you!"

"Oh, I'll be fine really. I'm praying you have a safe and fun trip!"

"Thanks," the pastor said, and with that he left.

Now, what was that all about, Trent thought, *I must look really worn out.*

Terry showed homes all afternoon to the young couple who wanted everything except the actual price tag. Frustrated, they called it a day and decided to meet again in the morning. Walking into her office, she headed straight for the coffee pot and poured herself a big cup of black coffee.

"You look a little stressed," her secretary said, and then laughed.

"I am," Terry said, frowning as she sat down on the sofa. "I had no luck finding the couple a house today, so I told them to go home and make a list of their absolute 'must have's' and where they could compromise. Hopefully tomorrow when we go out again they will have a more realistic picture of what they really need! Anyway, enough of that, I've got a closing at 5:30pm to get ready for, and after that I'm going home for a nice quiet evening!"

"What?" Kathy said, "Jeffery isn't on the agenda tonight?"

"No, he's out of town on business, and I'm taking advantage of it. Besides, I've got to work on my wedding invitations sometime."

"Want some help?"

"Sure, why not."

"So, when do you want me to come over?" Kathy asked.

"How about around 8:00pm. I need a little time to unwind with a nice hot bath."

"Sounds good," Kathy smiled. "In fact, I'll even order a pizza, and we can have girls' night out!"

"It's a date," Terry smiled, "and I won't even have to dress for the occasion."

"Me either," Kathy laughed!

Excited about having time alone, Terry opened the door and threw her shoes across the room. She headed towards the fridge and pulled out a water bottle. As she looked out her bay window she noticed the sun setting across the river, and the glistening buildings scattered across the skyline of the city. She just loved her condo, and secretly hated to give it all up when she got married. But Jeffery wanted to live in the suburbs, and have a big fancy house, and the white picket fence.

Thinking about that made her cringe, and she wondered if she could change his mind, at least for the first few years. She was a city girl at heart, and not ready just yet to have children and be bogged down with family responsibilities. She loved her real estate business and wasn't about to give it up and be a stay-at-home wife and mother ... not for the first few years anyway!

I just want to have some fun, not be bogged down, she thought. Just then she heard her phone ring, and knew it was Jeffery checking in.

"Hey Honey, how was your day?" Jeffery asked cheerfully.

"Oh, the usual," she said. "How about yours?"

"Good, I'm getting ready to go to a dinner meeting with a group of guys, but I wanted to check in with you first."

"Yes, I figured that," she laughed.

"So, what are you doing tonight?" Jeffery asked.

"Oh, I thought I would work on the wedding invitations, and my assistant, Kathy, is coming over to help!"

"How nice," Jeffery replied as he looked at his watch.

"Yes, I think she's bringing pizza over, so I won't have to order Chinese again."

Chuckling, Jeffery said, "Well, you two have fun, and I'll call you tomorrow before I fly out. Maybe we can have dinner tomorrow night?"

"Sounds good. Just let me know when you're coming in. I have to show houses to a couple all afternoon."

"OK, I shouldn't be too late, that is if the plane is on time; but I will call you either way. Guess I better go, or else I'm going to be late, but I'm missing you!"

As Jeffery hung up, Terry realized that she didn't miss him at all.

Chapter 8

Martha arrived home, late as usual, and grabbed a familiar frozen dinner from the fridge. Popping it into the microwave, she began flipping through her mail. Realizing there were more bills than anything else only stressed her more. Then she remembered the bottle of wine she had bought at her favorite store last week.

Looking in the pantry, she found it ready and waiting to be opened. She poured herself a big glass and flopped down on the sofa. Finding the news more distressing than her own life, she turned it off and closed her eyes to enjoy the silence.

It wasn't so long ago that she had enjoyed a social life with somewhere to go almost every night. Her pretty looks and fancy clothes had made all her friends jealous. *Where were they now when you really needed them*, she thought? *Lose the money, and the husband, and you lose their attention, I suppose*! She sat there fuming for a good half hour, then stood up and walked over to the window.

Raising her glass up towards heaven, she shook it, and found herself saying out loud, "It's not fair. It's just not fair! He should be the one suffering. Instead, he's married to a woman half his age, living in our house, and jet setting all over the world with his rich friends!"

She downed the rest of her wine in one swallow, tears streaming down her face, thinking, *who in the world am I talking to anyway? There's nothing, or no one out there who really cares.*"

Trent closed the door to his office after everyone left for the day. Sitting down in his favorite old chair he caught himself looking out on the big expansive lawn. It was a beautiful church, and he knew he was very lucky to be working there. But with a growing congregation comes lots of work, and problems ... suddenly the phone jolted him back.

"Hello, New Direction Church. How can I help you?"

"Honey, can you stop by the store and get some milk before you come home?"

"Sure," Trent smiled, "anything else for my beautiful wife?"

"No, can't think of anything," she said laughing. "Just seeing you soon is enough."

"I'm on my way,'" he replied and looked around to see if there was anything else he needed to do. Finding himself looking out the window again, he wished that he was the one going on vacation instead of Pastor Jeff.

Unforeseen

Henry cleared the kitchen table off and headed out to his beloved porch. He enjoyed hearing the birds chirp and listening to the children play in the neighborhood late in the afternoons. He wished little Stella was out playing, she really reminded him of his dear Marisa. He went into the den to grab his jacket lying on the couch when an envelope fell out of the inside pocket. Remembering the challenges they had been given, he tore it open and began to read. He had to catch himself or he would have fallen, and the tears streamed down his face as he read what his challenge was. What was the Lord doing, making him remember things so painful, and so very long ago?

Terry and Kathy munched on the pizza as they sat watching the moon come up slowly in the sky.

"Well, I guess it's time to start on the invitations. I've put it off all week long," Terry said, getting up to head towards the dining room.

"Yes, let's get it done. That way you can tell Jeffery that you were productive this evening," Kathy chuckled. "Wow, it looks like you're inviting half the city," she said, as she looked at the lengthy list

"That's actually Jeffery's list. Mine is over here! He has a big family and lots of friends and co-workers he wants to come. I don't. I really just want a few close friends to share in the day."

"So, are you excited about the wedding?" Kathy asked.

"I guess," Terry said hesitantly. "You know Jeffery, Mister Perfect. He has to have all his ducks in a row, and I'm the opposite. Spur-of-the-moment kind of girl. I fly by the seat of my pants!" They both laughed, as they began clearing the table.

"What's this?" Kathy pulled out an envelope that was lying near the invitations.

"Oh, that's the information I received at that mysterious inheritance meeting this morning." As she began opening and reading it, her face went ashen, and her head started spinning. The only thing she remembered was Kathy's voice asking her if she was OK.

Chapter 9

Claire looked at her watch and saw that it was already 8:45am, and still no one had arrived. Filling the coffee pot and putting the snacks out, she turned around to see Trent come in. "Why, hello!" Claire said, and reached out to shake his hand.

"Hi," Trent smiled and made his way to the coffeepot. Looking at the snacks, he took a couple of muffins and sat down. "Sorry, I didn't have breakfast this morning! I had an early morning meeting at the church."

"That's why I put them out," Claire smiled. "You are a youth minister, I believe?"

"Sure am," Trent said, "at a Church not too far from here, in the city center."

"I seem to remember it being called New Direction. Is that right? "

"Yes, it sure is. Have you ever visited us?"

"No, not personally, but I do have some friends that attend there."

"Really, what are their names?"

"Oh, you probably wouldn't know them. They are senior citizens, and don't get to go as often as they would like due to health issues."

Just as he was about to respond, Terry came running in. "Just made it," she said, a little out of breath, "but I see I'm not late after all!"

Claire smiled, and said, "No, it's not 9:00am yet. Make yourself a cup of coffee and fellowship a little."

"Actually, I need to speak to you if you have a minute."

"Sure, why don't you come to my office."

"Thanks," Terry said, as she threw down her heavy coat and took the envelope out of her pocketbook. Following Claire into the office, she remembered last night and the information that hit her like a tsunami.

"Um, I'm not sure how to say this," Terry looked at Claire. "Last night I opened up my envelope and read something quite surprising. In fact, I'm wondering how in the world this Mr. Peterson had knowledge of my life at such an early age? I don't know much about him, but it seems this inheritance deal is turning into something much more than money."

"Well, I can't say," Claire replied, "but I do know that he wouldn't do anything to hurt any of you. So, I would encourage you to stay in the group, and see how it all turns out in the end."

"I'm not sure I can do this," Terry said, tears in her eyes. "It's too painful, and I've got a lot on my plate already. You do know that I'm getting married in a few months, don't you?"

"No, I didn't know that! Congratulations," Claire said. "Perhaps this will help you in your preparations?"

"I don't know about that," Terry said slowly.

"Tell you what, you're here now, so why don't you stay? Then make your decision afterwards."

"Perhaps, but I'm not making any promises," she said, and turned around to go back into the room.

Claire watched her, thinking how pretty she was, and yet she seemed so troubled. Claire asked the Lord to please watch over Terry, and to help her to stay. With that she continued organizing her desk and hoped that Henry and Martha would be there soon.

Terry sipped slowly on her tea, looking at her phone, while Trent reached for another muffin. Martha walked in and laid her briefcase on the table beside Terry. "Thought I might be the last one to arrive," she frowned.

"Nope, seems to be Henry again," both Trent and Terry said at the same time.

"Today isn't a day that I can wait around for latecomers," she scowled.

Both Trent and Terry looked at each other and grinned.

"We are all on a schedule. What if we tell Claire that we can wait another five minutes then the meeting needs to start?" Trent suggested.

"Sounds good to me," Martha said, and made herself a cup of tea as well.

Henry got off the bus right in front of the Anderson building. Something told him to look up, but he walked quickly into the lobby instead. "Not sure I can continue doing this," he mumbled, "you've got to help me, Lord." He walked in as the meeting was about to start.

Claire handed them their journals, and asked if they had read their challenges. Trent and Martha had completely forgotten to read theirs, but Henry and Terry nodded, Yes.

Martha reached into her briefcase and found hers. However, Trent had no idea where his might be. While Claire went to find another copy for Trent, Martha quickly scanned her letter, and looked as if it were written by aliens from another planet. "They can't be serious, can they?" she said, turning to Terry

"What is it?" Terry asked.

"This challenge. They can't think that I am going to go to my ex-husband and tell him that I forgive him, can they? I mean, really, he's the one who walked out on me for a girl half his age! It will be a cold day in, well you know where, before that happens," and they both chuckled.

As Trent walked back in, he noticed the women were getting up to leave, their coats already on.

"Oh, is the meeting over?"

Henry spoke up and said, "I believe it is for the women, Son."

Just then Claire came back in and noticed all the commotion. "What's going on?" she asked.

"Well, we are leaving, as you can see," Martha spoke up.

"Yes," Terry said, "I need time to think before I can decide whether or not I want this inheritance that badly."

Henry agreed. "I have to side with the women on this also. I read my challenge yesterday, and I'm having second thoughts as well."

"I better open mine then and see what it says too. I'm curious to find out what all of you are talking about," Trent said. As he read the information he scratched his head and spoke up, "How in the world does this man know so much about us?" He continued, "And why is he playing God with our lives? He has no right to suggest anything to us."

"I know," Terry said, "and somehow he seems to know a secret from my past—one that I didn't even know. It's like he's some kind of fortune teller or something."

"I have to agree," Trent said, as he reached up to rub his forehead. "I'm a Christian, and I don't like someone I don't know trying to tell me how to live my life, except the Lord, and of course, my wife!" With that everyone chuckled.

"I can understand your shock and surprise, but did you read the whole contents of your envelopes?" Claire commented. "There also should be a part that tells how Mr. Peterson met each of you, and the impact you had on his life. If I were you, I would go home this evening and talk to your family. Pray, and then let me know in a few days what you decide, and if you are going to continue. Otherwise, I will need to cancel your part in this inheritance and give it to someone else."

They all agreed they would, and the meeting was adjourned.

Chapter 10

Shaking her head, Claire looked around the room after everyone had left—just not sure about the group. Picking up the unused journals that were left on the table, she finished cleaning the room. As she was shutting the door, she suddenly felt a desire to call Henry. Heading towards the office, she quickly dialed his number.

Henry heard the phone ringing as he opened the door. *Who could that be?* he thought, grabbing it. "Hello?"

"Hi Henry. It's Claire from the inheritance group."

"Well, hello," Henry smiled.

"Your name came to my mind a little while ago, and I was wondering if you would like to get together for a cup of coffee sometime soon?"

"Sure, I'm free as a bird these days," he chuckled. "What time were you thinking about?"

"How about tomorrow?" Claire said, looking quickly through her calendar.

"I'm up early," Henry replied, "how about 7:30 at that little diner beside your office?"

Unforeseen

"Sure, how do you know about that?"

"Oh, that used to be my hangout many years ago!"

"Well then, it's a date," she smiled. "Uh, I mean, I will meet you there tomorrow morning," she said, correcting herself.

"Sounds good. You have yourself a good rest of the day!"

Putting down the phone thinking, *now why in the world did I get so nervous? We're way past the dating age, for goodness sake!* As she straightened her desk she tried not to ignore the butterflies in her stomach.

Martha got to work with time to spare after the meeting. Sitting down at her desk, she started organizing her day when her boss came to her door. Looking up, she pretended not to notice his grin. "Yes, sir, how can I help you?"

"Well for starters, you can have dinner with me tonight."

"What?" She looked up quickly, only to see him coming towards her. "I told you, Mr. Williams, that I wasn't that kind of lady. I know how it is to be cheated on, and I wouldn't wish that on anyone's spouse!"

"Oh please, Martha, spare me the sermon. I love my wife too and wouldn't hurt her for the world, but a little late dinner isn't going to hurt either one of us."

"That's what they all say!"

"So, you're not going out with me?"

"No, not unless it's a company dinner, Mr. Williams." With that he turned around and headed back towards his office.

The nerve, she thought, as she shuffled her papers around. *I may not be religious, but at least I've got a conscience.* Distracted, she got up to pour herself a cup of coffee. *Maybe this will wake me up,* she thought. Then remembering the envelope with her challenge inside, she pulled it out and began to read it again. *It just doesn't make any sense that he would know about my personal life,* she mused. Putting the envelope away she tucked it under her papers.

"Everything all right?" she heard the familiar voice behind her.

"Of course, just reading something personal."

"I've got a meeting in five minutes. If you can prepare the affidavit for me, I will take it in with me."

"Sure, I'll have it ready in two minutes."

"Thanks," he smiled, giving her a wink. Looking down, embarrassed, a thought went through her mind. *Sure, he's a handsome man, rich and her boss, but he's also married, and I'm not going to get in the middle of that ... but what if?* Walking towards the conference room, she drove that thought right out of her mind.

Deep in thought about the challenge he had read earlier that morning, Trent gazed at the computer. *What have I gotten myself into?* he thought. *Why does this Mr. Peterson want me to take a sabbatical from the ministry for six months? The deacon board would laugh their heads off if I asked for six months off with pay! I'm a family man who needs to be more responsible than that ... and my wife ... that's a whole different matter. She's already stressed enough, working and being a mom and wife. I could just see her now, packing my bags and saying, "Honey, now you have a good time relaxing in that mountain cabin while I pay the bills, feed the baby, and take care of everything." Yeah right!*

Suddenly, laughing out loud, he looked up to see if anyone had heard him. He threw the envelope that held the challenge into the

Unforeseen

trash and continued working on the youth conference that was coming up in a few weeks.

Terry came in after the early morning meeting and laid down on the couch. Her head throbbing, she cancelled all her appointments and decided to take a mental health day. Closing her eyes, she again pictured her mom lying on a sterile bed trying to abort her ... As the tears flowed, she got up to get herself a drink of water.

Looking out her window she saw a mama bird hovering over her little one, feeding it a worm. Interesting she thought, *that bird shows more love than most humans.* Just then her cell phone rang, and she saw that it was her mom calling. Muting it, she threw the phone across the room.

Chapter 11

Startled, Terry woke up. It took her a minute to realize that someone was banging on her door. Before she could get up, Jeffery was already inside. "Are you all right?" He rushed over to her on the couch.

"Yes, I just needed a day off. I'm exhausted and had a bad day."

"Well, Honey, I called and called you, and couldn't get you. I started to worry because you always answer your phone."

She looked over at the broken phone lying against the wall and smiled. "I threw my phone across the room earlier today. Guess I broke it!"

"You think?" Jeffery picked up several parts of the phone. "What in the world happened?"

"I don't want to go into it right now, OK?"

"As long as I know you're all right," he frowned.

"I'm fine, really. So, are you hungry?" Terry asked, as she opened the refrigerator door.

"Yeah, I'm starving," Jeffery replied.

Terry got up to check her face, wiping herself with a cool cloth. "Well, do you mind getting take out? I really don't feel like going anywhere, and I don't have anything much in the fridge."

"No problem, I'll just go get us some sushi. Is that OK?"

"Sure, sounds good. I'll freshen up while you're gone."

"You always look beautiful, Honey!"

"You're a sweet man, Jeffery Barnes," she said, as she reached up to kiss his cheek!

"Well, I try," he grinned. "See you in a few minutes, and just try to relax, Sweetie. Tomorrow will be a better day!"

"I'm not so sure about that, but I hope so. It couldn't get much worse," she frowned.

Jeffery looked into her eyes that were so sad and wondered what in the world had made her so down. Hoping she would open up to him, he prayed a silent prayer for her as he turned to leave.

Henry always ate his dinner watching the evening news. Listening to all the politicians rant about the poor economy, he realized that the world was slowly becoming more and more like he used to be—selfish and greedy.

Knowing his time was shorter than most, he wanted to serve God the best he knew how. If this inheritance thing was something that the Lord had put in his path, then he knew He would confirm it to him somehow.

Suddenly, the meeting with Claire came to his mind, and he went over to his calendar to put down a reminder of their breakfast at 7am.

Trent drove into the garage and sat there wondering how in the world he was going to explain to Marcie about the challenge. As he came into the kitchen, he saw her cooking at the stove, and the baby sitting in the high chair eating.

"Well, hello, my beautiful wife and child!"

Marcie turned around and grinned. "Why, hello yourself! How was your day?"

"It started off quite interesting, then just became tedious."

"Really?" Marcie frowned. "What happened? Wait," Marcie stopped what she was doing. "Did it have something to do with your meeting this morning?"

Trent stopped playing with the baby and looked up. "As a matter of fact, it did."

"So?" Marcie waited to hear more.

"Well, it seems that to receive this inheritance money, each person is given a challenge of sorts."

"Honey, are you sure this is legitimate?"

"Oh, yes. I checked them out before I even went to the first meeting. However, this Mr. Peterson seems to know a lot about us for some reason."

"That's a little creepy." Marcie said, and turned around.

"Let's just relax." Trent smiled, helping her with the dishes of food. They prayed, ate, and then they talked throughout the night about the possibility of his unexpected sabbatical.

Unforeseen

As Terry washed the dishes, Jeffery suddenly came over to her and put his hand on her shoulder. "OK, Honey. I didn't want to bring it up while we were eating dinner, but I know something's going on."

Looking up, she replied, slowly, "Well, I found out some horrible news this morning at a meeting."

"What meeting was that?" Jeffery asked.

"You know, that inheritance meeting I told you about. Well, we have to meet six weeks before we receive it."

"That's crazy," he responded as he continued cleaning off the table. "Why in the world would you have to meet for six weeks? It should only be about a six-minute meeting with a lawyer!"

"Well, it's not. It's more complicated than that. It's not just about the inheritance anymore. Besides that, there are three other people involved."

"What? Well that means less money for you then, doesn't it?" Jeffery stopped and looked at her.

"Is that all you ever think about?" Terry asked him and walked over to the couch and sat down.

"What do you mean?" Jeffery responded a little defensively.

"Just what I said. Money seems to be pretty important to you."

Jeffery stopped what he was doing and looked at her.

"Honey, I love you. You know I do," Terry said, and got up to take his hand. "But I'm dealing with something right now that has nothing to do with money."

"I'm sorry, Sweetie," he said and took her in his arms. Hugging her tightly he continued slowly, "I know something bad has happened, I just wanted you to feel free to open up to me, that's all."

"I know," Terry said, as she laid her head on his shoulder, "I'm still trying to process it myself, but it's so difficult and painful that I can't actually put it into words yet."

They both sat down and began talking as the sunset fell across the patio, and the lights of the city slowly came on.

Chapter 12

Martha turned over to see what time it was. Stretching, and thanking the universe that it was the weekend, she got up from bed and stumbled over her purse lying at the foot of her bed. As she picked it up, an envelope fell out onto the floor. Fumbling around, she opened it and reread her challenge, once again surprised to see where she had met this Mr. Peterson.

She remembered that an old man had come by her office on the way from a meeting in her law firm. He had stopped by her desk. She acknowledged him but told him she didn't have time for small talk. However, for some reason she had offered him a cup of coffee. He accepted, and they ended up having a friendly conversation.

There was something different about him, she remembered—something very peaceful and serene. *I'm sure he was a nice man,* she thought, but there's no way on God's green earth that I will ever forgive my husband! This Mr. Peterson had no idea what I'd been though, nor my circumstances.

♦ ♦ ♦

Henry ordered a cup of coffee as he sat waiting for Claire. Looking at his watch, he noticed it was 7:00am sharp. *Pretty early to meet someone on a Saturday morning,* he thought, and he wondered again why she'd agreed to meet. Just then he looked up and noticed her coming in the door.

Waving, she nodded, smiled, and walked over.

"Would you like a cup of coffee?" he asked.

"Sure, that would be nice." He motioned for the waitress to come over.

"They have great waffles," he commented, "I usually splurge when I come here."

"Really?" Claire laughed. "I usually have the yogurt and granola, but why not?" So, they both ordered the blueberry-filled waffles.

"So, is it Miss Claire, or is it Mrs.?" Henry asked.

"Oh, it's Miss. I've been widowed for about five years now."

"I was just sitting here pondering why in the world an attractive lady like you would have agreed to have breakfast with me."

Claire smiled, then taking a sip of her coffee replied, "Well, I noticed on your information from the meeting that you were an architect at one time. Is that correct?"

"Yes, I was, but that was a long time ago," he chuckled.

Clearing her throat, she continued, "Am I to presume that you owned the Anderson building as well?"

"I did," Henry said, a little too quickly. "In fact, I owned several of them in my former life. But I was a different man back then. I do believe though that you already knew that since you know my last name is Anderson," Henry said grinning.

Unforeseen

"Is there something else you want to ask me?" he said, secretly hoping there wasn't a confrontation coming.

"Well, I wasn't sure, but now I'm pretty sure that my husband worked for your firm a long time ago."

"Really, what was his name?"

"Andrew Martin, but everyone called him Andy for short."

Looking down at his coffee, Henry nodded and said, "Yes, I knew Andy very well. In fact, he was a vital part of my team."

"Well," Claire smiled, "I had no idea that you were "the Henry" that he used to come home talking to me about every night."

"I hope it was good," Henry laughed.

"Oh yes, Andy liked you a lot. I guess I just pictured you a little differently in my mind."

"Well, I've changed a lot since then, and of course, gotten a lot older," he grinned.

"I had heard the Anderson building was supposed to be named after you," Claire added.

"Yes, they named it after me, even though I tried to vote it down."

"I see," Claire sat there idly stirring her coffee. She looked up and stared into his eyes, "So what changed in your life?"

As they sat there for what seemed like hours, he opened up and told her about his encounter with God, and how He had changed his life.

Later, Henry left the coffee shop whistling under his breath. *I haven't spent time with a woman like that in a long time* he thought, *but it sure does feel good! Sure wish I didn't have to wait so long to see her again.* Realizing what he was thinking, he shook his head and continued walking across the street to the bus stop, "I'm way too old for her," he mumbled to himself, "but I wonder if she would be open to at least going out to dinner with me one evening?" Shaking his head, he thought, *that will never happen since she knows about my past now.* Climbing on the bus, he sat in his familiar seat, looked out the window, and silently prayed for guidance from the Lord.

Terry woke up for the first time in twenty years without the feeling of suffocation, and she didn't remember dreaming that horrible dream either. It made her think that perhaps this newfound revelation was the truth after all, and that the reoccurring dream had something to do with her botched abortion.

But how did this Mr. Peterson know about what her mom had done almost 30 years ago? *And how am I going to talk to her about this?* Terry thought. She always knew there was something between them. She would sometimes catch her mom looking at her. Also, the coldness she had felt from her at times. Now it was all becoming too clear ... the rejection, and depression she struggled with most of her life. The need to always be perfect so people would love her—so that Jeffery would love her. She started to wonder if she was selling herself short by marrying him.

Grabbing her cup of coffee, she sipped slowly while looking out at the beautiful flowers she and Jeffery had planted in the spring. *Life is so fragile,* she thought. *One day you're beautiful and growing so gracefully, and the next day, you're a wilted flower ready to drop at any moment.*

Chapter 13

Henry came early before the meeting hoping to see Claire. Unfortunately, she was talking to Trent, who already had a cup of coffee in hand. "Well, hello there," Henry smiled at both of them.

"Hi," Trent said, shaking his hand.

Claire smiled and gave a gentle hug to Henry as she left them to get the snacks from her office. Trent noticed Henry turned to watch her leave. "So how are you Henry?" Trent took another sip of the hot coffee.

"Oh, I couldn't be any better," Henry grinned as he fixed himself a hot chocolate. "How about you?"

Trent nodded and said, "I'm fine."

"I don't hear a lot of enthusiasm," Henry said as he looked into Trent's eyes.

"Oh, I love my work, but I think I need a break. It's interesting that my challenge is to ask for a six-month sabbatical."

"Really?" Henry remarked. "Would your pastor and church be open to that?"

"Well, that's the rub," Trent responded, as he got up to grab a snack that Claire brought in.

Henry looked up to see Claire looking at him and winked. He noticed she blushed and walked back out the door.

"As I was saying, Trent continued, "it would be crazy for me to take a sabbatical—not just because of my work, but because of my responsibilities as a husband and a dad."

"Well," Henry said, "that's a sticky situation for sure. But if this is something that the Lord is directing you to do, then wouldn't it be irresponsible not to do it?"

"I suppose," Trent said slowly. "I know sometimes the Lord asks us to do hard things that don't make a lot of sense to us or to those around us. I guess I just need to pray for wisdom and direction to see if this is indeed from Him."

"That's right," Henry said, as he patted his arm. "I sure will be praying for you."

"Thanks," Trent said. "By the way, what's your challenge if I may ask?"

"Well, that's another story," he said vaguely.

"Oh, I'm sorry," Trent said, "didn't mean to pry."

"That's OK. It's just that I had a whole different life so long ago, and my challenge is confronting some issues. One of which is to get in touch with my children, whom I never see that much."

"Some reconciliation issues?" asked Trent.

"Yes, you could say that," Henry replied as he looked out the window.

"Well, I will be praying for you too," Trent said. He thought a minute, "This inheritance thing is turning out to be a lot more complicated than we thought, isn't it?"

As Henry looked to see the others walking in with Claire, he answered, "Sure is, Young Man, sure is."

As the meeting started, each person spoke about his/her individual challenges. Terry finally opened up and talked about the dream that had haunted her most of her life. Being a private person and describing her feelings was hard for her to do with strangers. She finally blurted out that she had just found out that her mother had tried to abort her. You could hear a pin drop—the room was so silent.

"Oh, my," Martha said, as she leaned forward, "what a horrible thing to have gone through! Do you think those dreams were because you actually remembered it in some way?"

"Perhaps," Terry said, looking around to see the expressions of everyone else.

A tear fell out of Henry's eyes, "So that's why you were so upset last week?"

"Yes, I opened my envelope to find out about this, and it threw me for a loop. I had to take the rest of the day off just to wrap my head around it."

"I can only imagine," Trent chimed in. "What a terrible way to find out. Have you spoken to your mom about this, or do you even have a relationship with her?"

"No and yes," Terry responded. "I haven't said anything to her yet, and I do see her occasionally. Let's just say that we have a cordial relationship at best. She's never really been a warm person to be around, and my dad left before I was born."

"Maybe that's why your mom did this—maybe she was feeling abandoned and rejected too," Martha commented.

"Maybe," Terry said, "but I've lived with rejection and perfectionism all my life, and I'm finally realizing why. I thought I was a mental case, but it's been her all the time. To tell you the truth, I'm mad, and angry, and if I say anything right now to my mom, it will be the wrong thing!"

"So, don't," Trent said, "I've got someone I want you to talk to. He's a counselor at my church. I think it would be good for you to talk to him first."

"Oh really?" Terry said frowning. "I guess I'm game for anything right now!"

"Great, I'll get you his contact information after our meeting."

As they continued talking, no one saw Henry slip out and walk into Claire's office. "Hello," he said peeking in.

"Why, hello yourself," Claire said, looking up from a pile of papers. "Are you all finished with your meeting?"

"I think we're almost ready to wrap it up, but I wanted a moment with you before leaving."

"Sure," Claire smiled. "Is there something wrong?"

"No, not so all," Henry said, as he stepped closer to her. "I was just wondering if you would like to have dinner with me sometime?"

"Why, I would love to," Claire smiled.

"Great," Henry said, "How about Friday night then?"

"Friday night? I've got plans already for that evening, but I am free on Saturday night. So, what would you think about me cooking you dinner?" Claire added.

"Really? Well now, I don't know of any man that can turn down a homemade meal from a good-looking lady."

Blushing again, Claire said, "I don't know if it will be good, but I will do my best to fill your belly!"

With that they laughed as they entered the room.

Chapter 14

Terry left the meeting feeling a little better, now that the truth was out. She hoped Jeffery would be as supportive as the others. Not that he didn't love her, she knew that, but he was usually so reserved about matters of the heart. Fumbling in her coat pocket, she found the name and number of the counselor Trent had suggested to her.

She knew she needed to talk to someone. So what if they were religious. If they didn't try to convert her, she would be open to any suggestions they may have. Reaching for her cell phone, she quickly dialed the number as she started her car.

"Hello," the man's voice sounded cheerful enough.

"Hello," Terry said, a little timid.

"How can I help you?" Ron continued.

"Trent, the youth pastor from your church, gave me your name. He said you were a counselor. Is that right?"

"Sure am," Ron replied. "Are you a member of the church here?"

"No, is that a problem?"

"Not at all," I was just checking. "Sometimes we have discounts for church members, that's all."

Laughing, Terry said, "No need for a discount for me. It probably won't take long, just wanted to talk to you about an issue that recently came to light."

"Give me a minute," Ron said grabbing his calendar, "how about tomorrow around 11:00am?"

"Let me see," Terry said as she hit her calendar app on the phone. "Looks like I'm free. Where are you located?"

As he gave her the address, she had a vague sense that this wasn't going to be as easy as she'd thought.

Trent sat at his desk fiddling with his pen, jotting down ideas for the youth retreat coming up in a few weeks. He found himself thinking about the sabbatical and all the things he could do if given one. *It's impossible*, he thought, *there's no way the pastor will ever give me that much time off. And I sure can't take it without pay. We just don't make enough.* Sighing, he continued planning the retreat.

Martha paced back and forth after she got home that afternoon. Feeling guilty that she'd said 'Yes' at a weak moment to dinner with her boss. So, what if she just wanted to go out and have a good time. *Nothing's going to happen, and I'm coming back home at a decent hour, by myself,* she thought. She admitted, *it almost felt good to be the "other woman" for a change. So then, why did she feel so uncomfortable?*

Unforeseen

As soon as she entered the restaurant she saw Stuart leaning against the bar having a drink. She waved nonchalantly, and he strode over to her with that easy smile, and those white teeth. "You're looking mighty good tonight, Martha," he said grinning.

"Why thank you, Stuart. I bet that's what you say to all the women. You do know you caught me at a vulnerable moment, don't you?"

Stuart shrugged, "One always seizes the day when one can," he said, with an easy smile.

She laughed as she thought, *At least I'm still noticed at my age.*

"Why don't we sit and wait at the bar?" he said and took her by the hand. "The waitress told me there's an hour and forty-five-minute wait right now."

"Why not?" she replied, as she let him guide her to an empty seat. As they were sitting and snacking on peanuts and martinis, he looked at her and said nothing for a long time. "What's wrong?" she said, as she took another long sip of her drink.

"I was just wondering what made you change your mind?"

"Like I said, you caught me at a weak moment."

Laughing he said, "OK, OK, I get it. I wore you down then?" Smiling her coy smile, she just remained silent. "So now you're playing hard to get, is that right?"

"One never knows, does one?" She grinned.

"Oh please, enough with the idioms," he moved in towards her, "let's make this a night to remember," Stuart winked at her. Nauseated, she looked away, suddenly regretting she had said 'yes' to him after all

Henry looked at Claire and all the food she'd prepared. "I'm so glad we're having dinner at your house, instead of some fancy restaurant," Henry smiled as he pulled the chair out for Claire at the table.

"Why, thank you, Henry. No one has done that for me in a very long time," she said, looking up at him.

He noticed her piercing blue eyes, and again thought how very attractive she really was. "You can't talk freely at those places like you can at someone's house," he replied.

"You're right," Claire said, as she looked around to make sure she had everything on the table.

"It sure smells good," Henry grinned as she passed him the fried chicken and mashed potatoes.

"Oh, it's just a little something that I whipped up," she said, and kept passing him bowl after bowl of steaming food.

"Now this is real eating," he grinned as he took a big piece of chicken. I might just have to have seconds," he commented.

"I sure hope so," Claire smiled, "but don't forget that I made dessert too!"

"You're spoiling me," he reached out and touched her hand ever so gently.

"Well, it's been way too long since I've cooked for anyone except myself, so guess I got carried away a little."

"That's all right by me," he said, as he ate a big spoonful of sweet corn. "I will gladly be your guinea pig anytime you want to cook!"

Laughing and enjoying each other at the table, neither one realized that they were falling in love.

Chapter 15

Trent knocked on Pastor Jeff's door first thing Monday morning after the pastor had returned from vacation.

"Come in," Pastor Jeff said, as he looked up to see Trent. "What's up, Son?"

"Well, didn't want to bother you so soon, but I have a question. Actually, a little story to tell you, if you have the time?"

"Sure," he said, as he put his pen down. "I've always got time for you!"

"Thanks," Trent replied, as he took a seat in front of the massive desk. "I trust that your vacation went well?"

"Sure did, I don't think I've relaxed like that in a long time. It was a much-needed break."

"That's great," Trent said smiling. "Because that's what I wanted to talk to you about this morning."

"OK," Pastor Jeff said, and pushed his chair back so he could really listen. "So, tell me, is everything alright, Son? You've seemed distracted lately."

"Oh yeah, everything is great. Maggie loves being a mom, and she juggles everything easily. The little one is growing so fast. I can't complain."

Pastor Jeff smiled and said, "That's good to hear. I know that my wife works harder than I do! Makes me feel guilty at times."

"Anyway," Trent continued, "I'm not sure if I told you what happened before you left a few weeks ago? Maggie and I were on our way to work one morning, and I got a phone call, out of the blue, from a lady saying that I had been given an inheritance from a man named Mr. Peterson. I told her I didn't know a Mr. Peterson, but she just went on to say there would be a brief meeting the following Wednesday about it. So naturally I went to see what it was about. Well, it turned out that there were three others, who had been given an amount too."

"So, was it a scam of some sort?" Pastor Jeff asked.

"No, it is legitimate. But there was a catch, which I should have known. Each of us were given individual challenges that we would need to complete to get our portion of the money. So, after I was handed an envelope, I found out what mine was."

"Really?" Pastor Jeff said, now sitting up, intrigued by it all. "So, what's your challenge, if I may ask?"

Clearing his throat, Trent said, "Well, that's why I'm here this morning, Pastor."

"Go on, Son, I'm waiting."

"Well," Trent said a little slowly, "I'm supposed to ask you and the church if I can take a sabbatical."

"A sabbatical?" Pastor Jeff repeated.

"Yes, a six-month sabbatical."

Pastor Jeff looked down at his desk, "I haven't even had one of those, and I've been here over ten years."

"I understand, Pastor." Trent looked at him, "I'm not sure why this is my challenge, and I feel foolish just saying it out loud, but I had to know if this was even a possibility."

Unforeseen

"Well," Pastor rubbed his face. "Trent, it's not up to me, but the board of deacons. All I can tell you is to write a letter to the chairman and ask them if they can discuss it at the next meeting. Tell me something, Trent. Are you feeling the need for an actual sabbatical, or do you just need the inheritance that badly?"

Trent sat there a minute trying to formulate in his mind the right words to say. "It's not that I need the money. The Lord is providing for me and my family. We are very happy here, and I love working at the church. But to be honest with you, I've been feeling dry lately. I can't put my finger on it, but everything I've been doing seems rote, and bland. I love the kids, and they're great. But I feel like I'm lacking the excitement and joy that I used to have."

"I see," said Pastor Jeff. "Tell me, Trent, how long have you been in the ministry now?"

"Well, let's see, I finished seminary about 10 years ago, and I worked part time as a youth and children's minister then. Then I worked at a church for three years as an Associate Pastor before coming here almost six years ago."

"So, in actuality you've been in the ministry for around 12-13 years?"

"That's correct," Trent responded.

Pastor Jeff got up and walked around his desk to be in front of Trent. Leaning on the edge of the desk he spoke slowly and looked intently into Trent's eyes. "I think what you are experiencing is burn-out. It happens to the best of us. In fact, I've experienced it too, right before coming to this church. I was seriously thinking about leaving the ministry and getting a secular job."

"Really?" Trent said, listening closely.

"Yes," Pastor Jeff kept talking. "Honestly, I'm not sure if the church will give you that amount of time off with pay.

However, if you asked for a couple of months, they may agree to it."

With that Trent looked down and saw that his knuckles were white. "Well, I only asked because of the challenge. What God does is up to Him. If I may ask you, Pastor, how did you get rested and renewed and able to keep on working in the ministry?"

"Well, that's another story that we need to discuss later. But for now, I will tell you this one thing. When you realize that it's not you who is doing this work—it's God doing it through you—when you see that your identity isn't wrapped up in the ministry, but only in Him, then your journey to healing and wholeness begins."

Trent nodded and pondered that insight, "Thank you, Pastor, for taking time to listen to me. I'll go back and pray about it as well."

"Glad I was able to help, Son, and let me know what you decide to do sooner than later, OK?"

"OK," Trent said, as he got up and walked out the door.

Chapter 16

Nervous and uneasy, Terry drove up to the church parking lot. She hadn't been inside a church since high school. Ringing the bell to the church office, all she really wanted to do was to run the other way, and then Trent appeared, smiling. "Well, hello," he said, as he reached out to shake her hand. "Come on in."

Trent showed her where to sit while he went to find Ron. As she waited, she noticed a missed call from her mom. *Glad I didn't hear her call*, she thought to herself, *that's the last thing I need right now*. Turning off her phone, she was putting it back inside her purse when Ron appeared around the corner. Surprised by his good looks and stature, she could hardly get her name out.

Smiling, he shook her hand, "I know people are nervous when they first come to me, but I haven't seen this response before!"

"Sorry," Terry blushed and straightened out her dress as she followed him towards his office.

"That's quite OK," Ron said, as he opened the door for her and sat down in his familiar leather chair. "Make yourself comfortable," he motioned her towards the couch directly across from him.

"I feel a little uncomfortable," she laughed nervously, "I've never been to a counselor before, especially in a church."

"I understand," Ron smiled. She noticed immediately he had a nice smile, and an easy demeanor that instantly made her comfortable.

"I am one of the pastors here at the church, but I am a counselor for all people."

Terry smiled. "Well, that's the reason Trent told me about you. Um," she paused for what seemed a long time.

"Take your time," Ron nodded.

"Well," she continued, "I recently found out something pretty awful." Ron smiled, and grabbed his notebook and Bible off his desk. Terry looked at the big black Bible. "You're not going to try to preach to me, are you?"

"No," he smiled. "But I do use it to give me help as I counsel those who come to me."

Terry cleared her throat and started explaining the unexpected inheritance and the challenge that went with it. "So, while I was in a meeting just a week ago, I read this challenge. Somehow the man who chose to give me money, also apparently knew something about my past."

"Oh, really," Ron said, as he stopped writing. "What was that?"

"Well," Terry stopped to gather her thoughts. "This man said that my mother tried to abort me, but apparently it was a botched one, because here I am!"

Ron looked intently in her eyes and said nothing for a moment. "Let me read something that I think might interest you." As he opened his Bible, he turned to Psalm 139:13-16.

> For you created my inmost being; you knit me together in
> my mother's womb. I praise you because I am fearfully and
> wonderfully made; your works are wonderful, I know that

full well. My frame was not hidden from you when I was made in the secret place, when I was woven together in the depths of the earth. Your eyes saw my unformed body; all the days ordained for me were written in your book before one of them came to be.

Suddenly it was as if the floodgates opened, and Terry could not stop crying. Ron got up to get some tissues and handed them to her.

She looked up, "I'm so sorry. I don't know where that came from."

"That's OK," Ron replied. "I believe God is comforting you and letting you know how very special and loved you really are."

"You think there is a God out there who formed us and loves us?"

"I sure do. If I didn't, then I wouldn't have any hope. I would always wonder why I'm really here in this world."

Terry just sat there trying to take it all in. She never believed there was a personal God, maybe some higher power, but that was all. "I never really felt loved as a child. I always felt an underlying disapproval from my mom. Oh, she wasn't mean to me, just distant. Now maybe I understand why. The thing is, I haven't talked to her since I found all of this out. I wanted to speak to someone to get some sort of perspective on it, you know."

Ron looked at the very pretty lady and saw a deep sadness in her eyes. "I understand," Ron said slowly.

Terry continued looking down at her hands. "She just called right before I came in. Thank goodness I didn't hear the ring. I don't like conflict, and I'm not sure how to even bring this up to her. Knowing her, she will probably just deny it."

Ron sat there for a minute, and then asked her, "Is your dad in the picture?"

"No, I never knew him," Terry spoke softly. "Mom wouldn't talk about him either. Perhaps he was the cause of her wanting to abort me."

"Well, I don't know that, and you don't either," Ron commented. "We may never know, but God does. He saw you before you were even born. And the reason you are still here today is that He has a plan for you far beyond your imagination."

"You really believe that? Terry asked, looking at him with her big brown eyes.

"I sure do," Ron said. "Let me make a suggestion to you." He leaned in. "Don't say anything to your mom yet. Let's continue processing your emotions and feelings for a few more weeks. Then pray about the right timing to reveal this. Is that all right with you?"

Moments passed by as she thought about it, and then she said, "OK, but I don't have a lot of time to wait."

"That's OK," Ron said, "I understand you are under a time crunch, but timing is everything to the Lord. Let's meet again next Friday, if that works for you?"

She picked up her purse and pulled out her phone. "I could meet between 3-5pm, if that's OK?"

He looked at his schedule and quickly marked it off. "Sounds good. Let's say around 4:00pm then."

As they both got up, he asked if he could pray for her, but she nodded and said, "No thank you. But thanks for your time."

"You're welcome," Ron smiled, and walked her to the door. As he watched her walk across the parking lot and get into her car, he silently prayed for her healing.

Chapter 17

Henry walked back into his house and sat down on the couch. As he sat thinking about his time with Claire, the challenge came back to his mind. Deciding to take the first step, he picked up the phone to call his daughter. A familiar voice answered the phone cheerfully.

"Hello?"

"It's me, Honey, your Dad. How are you?"

Silence greeted him as Marisa tried to gather her thoughts. "Pretty good. Glad to see you're using the phone I got you. So, how are you?"

Pretty good. So, how are you?"

"Doing well," she replied quickly. " Listen Dad, I'm going to be late for work. How can I help you?"

"Well, you were on my mind, and I just thought I would give you a quick call."

"Well, as much as I would like to chat, like I said, I'm running late today. Can this wait until another time?"

"Sure, I don't want to make you late for work. May I call again at a better time?" Henry asked hesitantly.

"Sure, why not. If I'm not home, just leave a message, OK?"

"OK, Honey. Hope you have a good day."

"You too," she said as she quickly hung the phone up.

"Well, that went well," Henry smiled a sad smile. Thinking out loud, he said, "I'm not sure that was such a good idea."

After collecting his thoughts, he picked up the phone again and called Claire, who cheerfully took his call, and they talked for a long time.

Finally, she said, "Henry, I do have lots to do today, but would love to see you again,"

"Well, funny you should say that, because I'm thinking we should go sailing this weekend. What do you think?"

"I would love to get out on the water! It's been a long time, and it's so relaxing! Do you have a sail boat?"

"Why, of course. There are lots of little surprises about me that you've yet to find out, My Dear," he said grinning.

"Well," Claire laughed, "you never cease to amaze me!"

"So, shall I come pick you up at 7:00am sharp on Saturday?"

"Of course," Claire replied. "I'll even make a picnic lunch for us to eat on the boat!"

"Sounds good to me. Now I can try out some more of your delicious food, can't I?"

"Absolutely, it will be a feast!"

"Well, see you then," Henry said. As he hung up, he noticed that his spirits were lifted.

Well, now that I'm on a roll, I might as well call David, and see how he's doing, thought Henry. As he dialed several numbers he had for David, he kept hearing a weird sound, and soon realized that the numbers had been disconnected.

Now where could he be? he sat there thinking. *I'll have to ask Marisa if she has his recent number the next time we talk.* Knowing David's addictions, and how often he'd changed jobs made him feel a little uneasy. *Oh Lord, please be with my David. He has so many problems. Let me get in touch with him soon!* he silently prayed. With that, he got up from the couch to start his day.

Martha arrived late to work. The weekend was a blur. She and Stuart spent every moment together. He had begged her to let him stay over, but she wasn't quite ready for that step, not for a while. Hating to admit it, even to herself, she was starting to like him, and that wasn't a good idea. She didn't like to be put into a vulnerable position, especially when it came to her personal life.

Suddenly the phone rang jolting her back to reality, and she heard Stuart asking her if she had plans for lunch. "No, but I am quite busy," Martha replied.

"Are you trying to get your work done in a timely manner?" Stuart said, laughing. "If so, you don't have to worry. I will give you time enough to work, just come with me today. I've got something very interesting to show you."

"Now, you have my curiosity up," Martha grinned.

"Great, that was my intention. So, shall I pick you up around 12:30?"

"Why not?" she said softly.

"See you then."

As Martha put the phone down, she couldn't shake that feeling she had when she rode a roller coaster as a child. The feeling of being high up in the air without having any control whatsoever.

Stuart arrived promptly at 12:30 as she was just coming out of the washroom.

"Well, you're always on time, aren't you?" Martha looked admiringly at his physique.

"Of course," Stuart grinned. "Let's go. We've got a lot to do in a short amount of time."

"OK," Martha, said grabbing her purse. "But what's the hurry?"

"I'm taking you to a building of mine that I want you to see."

"Really? Why? Do I need to get my real estate license now?"

Shaking his head, he said, "No, but you may need to get a mover very soon."

"What?" Martha gasped, and took a deep breath.

"Just calm down. I wanted this to be a surprise, but I've just leased you a penthouse apartment in one of my buildings, not too far from here."

"Why?" Martha looked dumbfounded.

"Because I wanted to, that's why," Stuart reached down to kiss her.

"I'm not, nor will I ever need to be, a kept woman. I do very well for myself, thank you very much." she said, and then she turned away from him.

He was silent for a moment, and said gently, "I know you are self-sufficient, Martha, I'm not doing this out of pity for you, but out of my love."

"Stuart, you're a married man. How can you love two women?"

"I don't. I only love you. The marriage I have with my wife is one of convenience only—it's been that way a long time."

"Then why not divorce her?" Martha replied.

"It's complicated." Stuart said, as he pulled out onto the freeway a little too quickly.

"Yes, that's what they all say," Martha smirked.

"Now, hold on with the attitude," Stuart said gruffly, "don't compare me to your ex-husband."

"Why shouldn't I? He had an affair with his secretary and my best friend. So, tell me what's the difference?"

Stopping the car quickly, Stuart grabbed her shoulders almost shaking her. "The difference is, I've been honest with my wife. I've told her about us, and my intentions."

Martha's face turned white, and she looked away from his gaze. "Why?" she said. "Why in the world did you do that?"

"Because as I said before, I love you, and I want to be with you. That's why I bought this condo for you!"

"I thought you said it was leased?"

"I only told you that, so I wouldn't scare you away. Now, are we going to see it and have a nice lunch, or are we going to fight the whole time?"

Martha slowly nodded, Yes, and Stuart pulled back out onto the freeway and continued on.

Chapter 18

Trent woke up early and looked at the clock; it was already 7:00am and the sun was up. Lying in bed, he yawned and silently thanked the Lord for having a day off during the week. He then remembered the meeting uptown. Turning over, he noticed that Maggie was up and already in the shower. Stretching, he sat up and grabbed his Bible to read a little before the baby awoke.

"Honey," Maggie said, as she jumped out of the shower drying off. " Can you fix me a strong cup of coffee?" She looked out of the bathroom while wrapping her hair up in a towel.

"Sure," he smiled, grabbing up his Bible, and planting a big kiss on his wife's cheek.

"What was that for?" she asked smiling her innocent smile.

"You just look too cute this morning," he grinned and winked at her.

"Well thanks," she said, as she started to apply her makeup. "So, what's your schedule look like today?"

"Oh, I've got that inheritance meeting at 9:00am this morning, but after that, I don't know." Trent started the coffee pot and put a bagel in the toaster. "Are you taking the baby over to the sitters, or do you want me too?" he asked.

"Oh, would you?" she replied. "That would give me a few extra minutes to have breakfast for once before I leave for work."

"Sure," Trent said and heard little Jacob start to cry in his bed. "Speaking of the little one, I think he's up!" Bringing the coffee to Maggie, he bowed slightly and said, "Here my Love, made just for you!"

"Why, thank you, Sweetie. This is already turning out to be a great day! So glad you're off; you need to do it more often," she commented.

"Wish I could, but only when I have a full weekend do I get these little perks!" Trent turned and headed off towards Jacob's room as the crying was getting louder and louder.

"Hey, now, Little One, I'm here. Just calm down." Jacob looked up with a tear stuck on his long dark eyelash. "Aren't you a rascal?" Trent said, as he scooped him up and gave him a big bear hug! Laughing, Jacob grabbed a hold of Trent's beard before he could stop him.

"Ouch," he said as he took hold of Jacob's little hand. "You are a strong one, aren't you?" He reached down to kiss him on his fat little cheek. "Lets you and I go get some breakfast, what do you say about that?" Jacob giggled, and off they went to fix peanut butter and jelly toast.

"So," Maggie said, as she grabbed a half of a bagel and smeared some cream cheese on it. "Have you heard anything about your sabbatical yet?"

"No, the meeting is on Sunday afternoon at five, right before worship the service. I should know something that evening."

"Are you nervous?" she asked, while sipping her coffee.

"Well, I am, and I'm not. All I can do is ask, like the pastor said. And the rest is in God's hands. If He wants me to do this, then I believe He will allow them to make the right decision. If not, then what have I really lost? An inheritance that I had no idea existed, or how much it really is?"

"You're right," Maggie smiled. "What do we have to lose? Well, I'm off to work, Honey. Thanks so much for taking Jacob. I'll call the sitter and let her know you're coming, and that you'll be a little late."

Trent got up from the table and gave her a hug. "Hey, why don't we go out for dinner tonight? Just you and me."

"Really? That would be great!"

"I'll see if one of the kids from church can come over and babysit for us. They need to make some money for their mission trip. Anyway, it's going to be a surprise for you. Just wait and see," Trent smiled and watched her head out the door for work, not realizing in just a few short hours his whole world would change.

Terry's phone vibrated in her purse as she pulled out of the church parking lot. Looking down, she saw that it was her mom again. "Guess I can't avoid her forever," she mumbled, hitting her redial.

"Hello, Honey. Is that you?"

"Yes, Mom. Sorry I couldn't get to the phone in time."

"Are you all right?" her Mom's concern was evident. "I've called several times this week, but you didn't answer."

"Yes, Mom, I'm fine. Really no need to panic. I've just been busy with the wedding, and some other things that have come up recently."

"Is it work, Dear? Because if it is, perhaps I can come down, and we can take a few days off to go to the beach house? I haven't

Unforeseen

been there this summer, and that would give me an excuse to spend some time there with you!"

"No, Mom. It isn't work. That's going fine, but the beach does sound inviting."

"That's great, Honey. When shall I come down to get you?"

"I'm not sure." Terry suddenly had second thoughts. "Before we make plans, I'll need to check my work schedule and get back with you. How about if I call you later, after I get home?"

"That's fine, just let me know, and I will have the maintenance man open the house up and get it ready for us!"

"OK, Mom. Listen, I've got to go, but we'll talk later this evening."

"OK, Honey. Glad you're OK. I was worried."

As Terry threw her phone back into her purse, she panicked for a second, not wanting to spend that much time alone with her mom. But then she remembered her counselor's wisdom about timing. *Not exactly relaxing, but it will give us that time alone,* she thought.

Chapter 19

Stuart pulled up to the gate which led into the pricey high-rise condominiums. The sun glistened on the rooftops of the penthouses. Martha's mouth dropped open as she realized this man's intentions towards her. Squirming in her seat, she pulled her coat a little tighter as he pulled into a parking space in front of one of the more beautiful buildings near the back area.

"Wow," Martha said slowly, "I had no idea you were bringing me here today!"

"Well, then I've surprised you," he said smiling.

"Yes, I have to admit, you sure have!" Martha said as she kept looking at the expansive building with the beautiful lake views.

"Let me continue then," he grinned, as he pulled out two new shiny keys. "This key is for the building and this one is for your new penthouse apartment."

"Uh, you bought me a penthouse condo?" she said a little too loudly?

"Yes, nothing is too good for my girl" he looked at her intently.

Her hands were shaking as she put the key into the new lock. The door opened effortlessly, and she looked into the corridor that was lined in gold and rich dark wood. "This is beautiful," Martha said as she gazed around to see that each condo had a separate entrance. "Yes, it is high end and state of the art, all built with privacy in mind."

"I can see that," Martha mumbled as they rode the glass elevator up to the penthouse. She couldn't look at Stuart because he began to make her feel uneasy.

"Well," Stuart smiled, "this is it!"

Martha opened the door slowly that led into the 2000 square foot apartment which overlooked the lake. "Oh my!" she put her hands up to her mouth, "I don't know what to say."

Before she could say another word, Stuart took her into his arms and gave her a long lingering kiss. "You don't need to say anything, except thank you," Stuart grinned and took her hand that led to the master bedroom.

"Look at this view," he said as he pulled open the wooden blinds. Martha's head was spinning. "And look," Stuart continued, "at the private terrace you have where you and I can enjoy long evenings together. That reminds me," he said "let's go into the kitchen. I've got something for us to enjoy."

"There's more?" Martha asked as she followed him into the expansive great room that led to the kitchen. She stopped mid-sentence, "This is a chef's dream kitchen!"

"It sure is." He turned around and opened the fridge. Inside was a chilled bottle of champagne and some cheese and crackers.

"Well, you certainly thought of everything, didn't you?", Martha said, as she walked towards the quartz island.

"I try," Stuart replied, as he gave her the chilled glass. "Let's toast to our love that hopefully will last for many years to come." As she took a sip, she felt a knot form in her throat. She wondered if she could do this after all.

After what seemed like hours, they ended up on the couch together. Things had happened so fast, it almost seemed like a dream, and she was watching it all in slow motion. Suddenly sick to her stomach, she ran into the bathroom sweating. "What's wrong?", Stuart got up and buttoned his shirt running his fingers through his hair.

"Nothing" she said, as she splashed her face with cold water and checked to see if she still had some lipstick on. "Just had to get some water, I felt a little faint—probably from all the excitement—and the champagne on an empty stomach too."

"Oh well, I can fix that. I made lunch reservations not far from here. Let's go, and then we can discuss when you want to move in here." As they left the condo, she turned around once again to admire the view. Just then she noticed a couple pull up next to her building. Getting out, they walked into the massive foyer smiling. *Um, bet they're married* Martha thought, as Stuart opened the door for her to get into his car.

Sitting outside at the yacht club they looked out over the water and talked about the future.

Later that afternoon when Martha finally got back to the office, she sat down at her desk and put her head in her hands. Suddenly she felt nauseous again and got up to get a cold glass of water.

What in the world am I doing, she thought. *I've become my husband! And for what, a beautiful condo downtown, and fancy dinners? What's gotten into me? Can I be bought that easily?* As she scrolled through her calendar on her phone to see what was on the agenda for tomorrow, she realized that she had another inheritance meeting, and she groaned out loud. The last thing she wanted to do was talk about forgiving her ex-husband. Right now, she couldn't even forgive herself.

Unforeseen

Trent was putting Jacob into his car seat as someone pulled up behind him in the driveway. Looking up to see who it was, he saw the flashing blue lights and wondered what in the world was going on. Hearing someone clear his throat, and he looked up to see the policeman towering over him.

"Are you Mr. Williams?"

"Why yes, I am. What seems to be the problem?"

"Well, it looks as if you're going somewhere?"

"Yes, as a matter of fact, I was getting ready to take my son to his sitter, but I'm in no hurry." As Trent rounded the front of the car, he noticed another officer, a lady getting out of the front passenger seat. "Has something happened?" Trent suddenly had a sinking feeling.

"Well, Mr. Williams."

"Just call me, Trent," he interrupted him.

"To answer your question, Trent, yes. Your wife was in a hit and run accident this morning, and we are here to escort you to the hospital where she's being tended to."

"She's not dead, is she?"

"I can't say, Trent, but I do know she was transported by ambulance and is in the E.R. right now. I'm sure the doctors on call will fill you in with all the details. So, if you don't mind, let's take your child to the sitters and head on over there."

Trent felt the urgency from the officer's voice, and quickly strapped Jacob into the car seat of their car. He found himself praying silently on the way.

Seeing the hospital up ahead, Trent wasn't listening to the policeman, and he had no idea what he had just said. All he wanted to do was to get to the E.R. and see how Maggie was.

He kept mumbling over and over again, *Lord, please, please let her be alright, I don't know what I would do if something happened to her.*

As they pulled around to the E.R., Trent jumped out before they could say goodbye. Then he remembered to turn around to say, thank you. They handed him his car seat and nodded to him. Running into the lobby, he looked for someone to ask directions of when suddenly he saw a young nurse coming his way. "Miss," he said as he grabbed her hand, "can you tell me where my wife is?"

"What's her name?"

"Maggie, Maggie Williams. She came in a little while ago. She was in a car accident. The police just escorted me here."

With that, the nurse ushered him over to a small waiting room and told him to wait, she would try and get some help. Trent sat there wringing his hands and praying, *Oh Lord, please, please don't let me lose my Maggie, please. She's my life next to You. Please don't let Jacob lose his mother.*

Just then he saw the doctor come out of the E.R. and take off his bloody gloves. Reaching out to shake Trent's hand, Trent could see tears in his eyes. "Are you Mr. Williams?"

"Yes, is Maggie OK?"

"Well, your wife has some serious injuries, but the thing we are most concerned with is her head trauma. She's in an induced coma right now, and we are evaluating her. We don't want to risk more swelling."

Suddenly Trent went weak at the knees and the doctor ushered him over to a chair. "Do you need me to call someone for you? Is any of your family in the area?"

Trent nodded and said "Yes."

"Good," the doctor replied. "Can we call them for you?"

"No, I'll take care of it."

Unforeseen

As the doctor sat down to explain the rest of Maggie's problems, Trent could only think about the possibility of losing the love of his life.

Chapter 20

Claire walked into the room where everyone was gathered around the coffee pot, except for Trent, which was very unusual. Looking around she asked if anyone had heard from him.

Henry spoke up and said, "No, but I'll give him a call. He gave me his cell phone number last week."

"I think I have it too," Terry said, as she scrolled down her recent number list. "Here it is Henry, if you need it."

"Thanks," he said as he prayed silently that nothing would be wrong. After five rings, the voicemail picked up, and he left a quick message.

"Well, let's get started," Claire said. "I'm not sure if you picked anyone to take notes for these meetings, but if not, it might be wise to do so. That way you will know what's taking place every week. This is your third time, and you all are already half way through."

"Well," Henry said laughing, "I better leave the note taking to the ladies. I have terrible handwriting."

Martha spoke up, "Just because we're women, doesn't necessarily mean that we are better secretaries, if that's what you're saying?"

"No, no," Henry said quickly, "I just meant to say I don't have good penmanship, that's all."

Claire sighed and turned to go to her office. Shaking her head, she thought Martha was one defensive lady!

Terry grabbed her notepad, "I'll do it. Don't mind at all."

"By the way," Henry said, "before we start, I would like to say a quick prayer for Trent. Something just tells me he needs it right now."

Feeling a little silly about her outburst, Martha closed her eyes and listened to the old man pray like he was really talking to someone personal in the room.

Pastor Jeff found Trent standing over Maggie sobbing. He quickly grabbed his arm and escorted him out into the hall.

"Son, do you need someone to pick your little boy up?"

"What?" Trent said, not really looking into the pastor's face.

"Is your son going to need picking up?"

"No, the sitter knows that Maggie was in an accident, and they're taking care of Jacob today."

"OK, then, let's go sit somewhere and talk just a minute."

"I don't want to leave Maggie," he pulled away from him and walked back to the room just as the nurse came in to take her vitals. Pastor Jeff wiped the tears from his face and took Trent's hand to lead him back out into the hall, away from the nurse.

"Let's sit down and take a deep breath and pray."

"Pray? I prayed all morning and didn't hear anything except the doctor saying she was in a coma, and they don't know anything else right now."

"Trent, the Lord is right here with you, even if you don't hear, see or feel Him. He hasn't forsaken you, not one minute. He's also with Maggie now, and she's in His hands."

Trent shook his head, turning away. Just then he saw Maggie's mother and father walking into the room. She ran towards Trent and grabbed him tightly. "What happened?" she said as the tears came.

"Is she all right?" Maggie's father asked.

Pastor Jeff spoke up, "She's in an induced coma, and they're watching her."

"Where is she?" Maggie's mother asked as she looked at the Pastor.

Pastor Jeff took the couple and escorted them to Maggie's room. Suddenly Trent felt his phone vibrate. Grabbing it, he noticed there was a voicemail. Walking over to the window, he listened to Henry's message that he had left a few minutes ago.

"Oh no, the meeting," he suddenly remembered, I forgot all about it. Guess I need to let them all know what has happened."

Henry heard his phone ring and grabbed it before anyone else noticed. "Excuse me," he said to the ladies, walking out the door.

"Hello, Henry? This is Trent. I just saw your message."

"Son, I called because we were worried. You're always here before anyone else. Is everything OK?"

"No, Henry. It's not. My wife was in a hit-and-run accident this morning, and she's in critical condition." Henry couldn't speak for a minute.

"Are you there, Henry?"

"Yes, Son I am. Is there anyone with you?"

"My pastor and Maggie's parents are here. Mine are on the way, but they live out of town."

"I'm so sorry, I don't know what to say."

"Well, if you will just let Claire and the ladies know, I would appreciate it. I'm not sure if I will be able to continue with the meetings, but I'll let you know."

"Know that we will be praying, Trent. If there is anything I can do, please don't hesitate to call me!"

"Sure," Trent said as he hung up the phone, and turned around to return to Maggie's room.

Henry walked into Claire's office and knocked lightly. Claire looked up, smiled, then noticed Henry's white face. "What's the matter?" she stood up and walked over to him.

"Trent just called me back. He said his wife was involved in a hit-and-run accident this morning, and she's in critical condition."

Claire leaned back against her desk and couldn't speak for a minute. "Oh my, we really need to go to see him. Why don't we all go over to the hospital and let him know we are here for him?"

"Sounds good," Henry agreed, "let's go tell the others."

Terry called into work, said she had an emergency, and Martha quickly called Stuart to let him know that she would be late. They all rushed over to the hospital, but as soon as they walked into the waiting room, they saw Trent with a group of people around him.

Henry spoke quietly to Claire, "Well, at least he's not alone."

Claire looked at all the people, "Perhaps we should just pray with him and then leave."

"I agree," Henry said as they inched closer.

Just then Trent happened to look up and see them. Smiling ever so slightly, he waved them over and begin to introduce them to the others. "Thanks guys for coming. This is so thoughtful of you all."

"Well, we wouldn't have had it any other way," Henry smiled a sad smile, "just wish it was under better conditions."

Trent shook his head and a tear fell down his cheek. "She's a strong woman. I was planning on taking her out tonight for a fancy dinner. She works so hard."

Claire nodded and smiled. "Can we do anything for you?" Terry said and glanced over to Martha.

"No, I can't think of anything right now, except your prayers, of course."

"That goes without saying," Henry said, as he grabbed ahold of Trent's hand. In fact, can we all pray a quick prayer with you now?"

"Sure," Trent said, as he moved away from the others towards a corner of the room. Claire quickly took Trent's other hand, and Terry and Martha stood awkwardly behind them with their eyes closed.

Looking up after their prayers, Trent said, "Thank you," and he reached out to hug Henry. "Without the Lord I would never be able to make it through. He is indeed my hope."

Both Henry and Claire nodded and agreed. As they left, Martha began to think that there just maybe something or someone out there in charge after all.

Chapter 21

Trent realized he had been sleeping for several hours beside his wife's hospital bed. What had awakened him? Hearing a low moan, he jumped and knew it was Maggie, he would know that voice anywhere.

"Nurse, Nurse," he screamed.

Suddenly there were nurses everywhere, pushing him out of the way. They checked her vitals, but everything seemed to be all right.

"So why was she moaning?" Trent asked.

One nurse motioned for Trent to step out of the room with her.

"She's not responsive. It probably was just a reflex action. Many times, people in a coma may move, turn their heads, mumble, and you think they are waking up. But brain injuries are complex, and everyone is different. It just takes time. Talk to her and see if she'll respond to you, but don't be discouraged because it may be a slow process."

He began talking slowly at first. Then he started telling her about Jacob and what he did the other day. Soon he was laughing and crying all at the same time. Maggie began moaning again and seemed to try to open her eyes. But just as quickly, she fell silent again.

Dr. Williams came by later that evening and explained the process they called "emerging". It's when the patient takes small steps of waking up, a little at a time: first with eye movement, then speech, then leg and arm movements.

"But I thought the medicine you gave her to induce the coma was out of her system already," Trent said.

"Well, the swelling in her brain may be affecting her ability too; we just don't know yet. The brain is a complicated organ, one that still amazes us. For now, Mr. Bowers, why don't you just go home to your little boy, rest, and get a change of scenery. We will let you know if anything else takes place."

Trent turned to go, but he looked at Maggie one more time, silently praying that the Lord would allow her to live and get better. Grabbing his coat, he walked down the long corridor towards home.

Terry drove to the church for her second session with her counselor. She was glad she had someone to talk to after such a tragic week. The nagging thoughts about Maggie were consuming her. Maybe Ron would have an answer that made sense to her. *If God is such a loving God, then why would He let a wife, and mom almost die in a car wreck?* she thought.

As she walked down the hall, she noticed Trent's door was open, and she peeped in. It took her by surprise to see him working at his desk. Looking up from his computer, he recognized her. "Hi," he said, motioning for her to come in.

"I didn't know if you would be working today or not," Terry smiled.

"Just came from the hospital this morning, still no change. The doctor told me it may be a while before we know anything. So, I'm trying to catch up on some work. But the good news is it seems Maggie's trying to wake up, she's making a lot of moaning noises."

"That's good news, isn't it?" Terry commented.

"I think so by the way the nurses and doctors responded, but they said brain injuries are complicated and each person is different. So, it may still be some time before they know what damage, if any, Maggie may have."

"I can only imagine what you must be feeling," Terry just stood there awkwardly.

"Well, it's not easy, but the Lord is seeing me thorough."

"Like I said before, if there's anything I can do ... "

"Thanks," Trent said, a little too quickly, "but all I need right now are your prayers."

"Well, I'm not sure if I'm the best person to do that, but I will try," Terry grinned. "Guess I better get going. I will see you next week at the meeting, right?"

Thinking a minute, "Oh, that meeting. Well, I'm not sure about that, but I'll see," Trent replied.

Terry continued towards Ron's office, wondering how she was going to bring up the subject of God today. Before she knocked on the door, Ron opened it to let her in.

"Have a seat anywhere; would you like a cup of coffee or bottled water?"

"No thanks," Terry said, "I just had a quick bite to eat before coming."

"Great, so tell me how have you been?"

"Well, let's just say, it's been a hard week."

"Yes," Ron said, "sadly, we were all stunned to find out what had happened to Maggie. I would be devastated if that happened to my wife."

"Oh, you're married?" Terry asked.

"Sure am, for 20 years now."

"Wow, and I thought you were younger than I was!"

"No, but I think I do look young for my age!" he responded laughing.

Laughing broke the tension, Terry felt.

"So," Ron continued, "have you been able to speak to your mom yet?"

"No, but we've talked, and I plan to see her this weekend. Pray for me, please. This isn't easy, even in the best of times."

"I understand," Ron replied. "We will pray about it before you leave today. So, let's talk about all the possible outcomes that could take place, and how this might impact your relationship."

"Well," Terry said letting herself relax a little, "we don't have the closest relationship. So worst case scenario, it would completely ruin what little we have now."

"I see," Ron said. "But how is this news affecting you? Are you still having those disturbing dreams?"

"Actually, I'm not. In fact, they stopped the moment I found out the truth!"

"Interesting," Ron said smiling." I had a feeling they just might."

"Really, why?" Terry leaned forward.

"Well, there's a verse in the Bible that says, 'The truth will set you free'."

"Where's that?" Terry frowned.

"Well, let me find it. Do you have a Bible at home?"

"No, I used to have one somewhere, a little children's Bible that I got one Easter Sunday when Mom and I decided to go to church."

"I see. Well, I tell you what, I will give you one before you leave today, just remind me."

Terry smiled and thought to herself, *here we go pushing religion on me*, but she bit her tongue.

"Here it is," Ron pointed to the verse that was in the New Testament. It's in John, 8:32, "Then you will know the truth, and the truth will set you free."

Terry just sat there quietly, then said, "So how do you know that the Bible is really true?"

"Well," Ron leaned back, his hands near his chin. "Historically, the Bible is the most well-documented book that has ever been written. But I believe most importantly, it validates itself."

"What do you mean?" Terry replied.

Ron continued, "With all its different authors writing at separate times and centuries, but they all say the very same thing about God, prophecies, miracles and teachings. Well, mathematically this is an impossibility."

"I see," Terry said, not wanting to get too deep. "I've been thinking there must be something, or someone, out there who made all this, who made us—or else I wouldn't even be here. I mean, my mom tried to kill me, and I didn't die. That says something doesn't it?"

"It sure does," Ron said, "It says that life is valuable, that you are valuable. That the God of the universe has a plan for your life, and He meant for you to be born at this very time, in this very place. Nothing is an accident with the Lord."

"Well, that's a lot to think about," Terry nodded ready to change the subject. "But why would He allow a terrible thing to happen to Maggie? I mean if He is in control and really loves us like you say He does?"

Ron then begin to explain how Jesus came, died, and rose again, and because of this we can have new life and a new beginning—one that never ends, even when our physical body dies.

"That's a little heavy," Terry commented.

"I understand, and it's something we can continue discussing as you have questions," Ron added.

"OK," Terry said hesitantly. "Well, I will let you know next week what happens this weekend with Mom. And yes, you can pray for me if you would like," Terry smiled.

"In fact," Ron got up and walked over to her chair, "if I could, I would like to end this session today with a quick prayer."

"Sure, I guess so," Terry nodded, and as they bowed their heads, she felt the very same feelings she had that morning when they'd all prayed for Trent's wife in that cold sterile hospital waiting room.

Chapter 22

Henry took a sip of his coffee and thought about his children. He missed them, and knew it was time. Time to make plans to see them. So, sitting there at the breakfast table, he began to map out the destinations and to make travel arrangements. First, he thought he would fly in to see his older son in New York, then from there take a train to Chicago where his daughter lived, and then fly down to Mexico where his youngest son was supposedly staying with some friends.

Looking at his calendar, he thought about leaving on Thursday after the meeting. That way, he could let them all know what he was doing and ask for prayers. He also wanted Claire to know. In fact, he smiled, wouldn't it be nice to have her come along with him. He smiled as he sat there thinking— It sure would be an adventure that they could share together!

But first things first, he thought, I need to call Trent to see how he's doing. Just can't imagine how he's coping right now. Reaching for his phone, he dialed his number praying silently for the right words.

"Hello," Trent said sleepily.

"Trent, I hope I didn't wake you?"

"Who's this?" Trent said a little gruffly.

"It's Henry, Son, just wanted to check on you and see if there was anything you needed."

"Oh, Henry, Sorry, I'm not myself today. Didn't sleep at all last night. Just put Jacob back to bed, then I went back too."

"That's all right, Son, I'm sorry I called so early. I would really like to come over today and maybe take you and Jacob out to lunch. I've got some business in town this morning."

Hesitating, Trent said, "I've not been real hungry lately, and I'm not sure you understand what it's like to take a toddler out to eat!"

Laughing, Henry said, "Well, I know it's been a few years, but I seem to remember how that works. But maybe I could just pick us up a sandwich or something and bring it over. Would that be easier?"

"Yes, I think so, Besides I'm not sure if I'm up to going out right now. I'm not real good company."

"That's ok, Son, I may see if Claire wants to come with me, if that's ok?"

"Sure, why not, I think Jacob would like to see a woman in the house. He's really missing Maggie. He may be small, but I think he knows something isn't quite right."

"Well children are more perceptive then we realize," Henry replied. "OK, then, I will let you go back to sleep, and I will see you later today."

"Thanks, Henry. You're a thoughtful man."

"I try Trent, but I've got a long way to go."

"Don't we all," Trent said, and hung up the phone.

Well, I might as well take another step of faith, Henry thought to himself. He then took his cell phone out of his pocket, and dialed Claire.

"Hello," Claire said cheerfully.

"Well, hello yourself," Henry chuckled. "You're certainly in a good mood today!"

"Yes, it's a beautiful day, and I'm feeling great. What more do I need!"

"You're right," Henry replied. "When we can open our eyes, get up out of our beds and walk—then that's a gift from the Lord, isn't it?"

"Sure is," Claire chuckled. "So, Henry what are you calling me about so early this morning?"

"Well first off, I just got off the phone with Trent, and I'm going to take lunch over to him today, and wondered if you would like to come with me?"

"I would love that. I've been thinking and praying for him a lot these last few days and wondering how he was doing."

"Well, I don't think he's sleeping much, not sure if it's the baby, or just stress."

"Maybe a little of both," Claire said.

"Yes, you're probably right. So, can I pick you up around 11am? That way we can grab some food, then head on over?"

"That sounds great!"

"Good, because I've got another proposition to talk to you about later."

"Really?" Claire laughed. "You are full of surprises today aren't you Mr. Jamison, or shall I call you Mr. Anderson now?"

"You can call me anything you would like as long as it involves food!" Henry chuckled. Closing his phone, he smiled, and looked out at all the beautiful flowers that lined his sidewalk, and said a quick prayer for wisdom, and guidance.

◆ ◆ ◆

Martha was changing. She could tell her heart was getting softer, especially after Maggie's accident. She wasn't thinking about her ex anymore, and she seemed more content. She was even looking forward to the meeting tomorrow and seeing everyone. But as her heart became softer, she became more uncomfortable in her relationship with her boss. Sitting at her desk that morning she twiddled her pen and stared off into space.

What am I going to do? she thought to herself. *I've got to get out of this, but how? I can't afford to lose my job, not right now.* Just then Stuart peeked around the corner and smiled as he walked towards her desk.

"Hi beautiful," he said and leaned across to kiss her.

"Hi," Martha said without smiling.

"What's wrong, you seem distant," Stuart frowned as he sat down in front of her.

"Oh nothing, I've just got a lot on my mind this morning."

"Well, maybe this news will perk you up! I've got an upcoming business trip to Las Vegas in a couple of weeks. I was thinking it would be a nice trip for the two of us?"

"I don't know Stuart. Let me think about it OK?"

"What's there to think about?" Stuart said.

"I don't know. All I know is that I need some time to think about it ok?" Stuart sighed, "So what's really going on Martha? I know something's up."

"Well, I know you say your wife knows about us, but that doesn't mean she approves. Nor does it mean she's not hurt over it. If she didn't love you, she would be gone by now, don't you think?"

"Not necessarily," Stuart said without emotion. "She knows which side her bread is buttered on, and she doesn't want to lose her social standing in the community either. That's everything to her."

"So, she's willing for you to be unfaithful, just to keep the money and status?"

Unforeseen

"Yep, that about sums it up," Stuart said, as he grabbed Martha's hand and kissed the top of it. Martha jerked her hand back from his, and just stared at him.

"Well, call it a conscience, but I'm feeling a lot of guilt, and I don't know if I can continue seeing you. I just need some time to think. Why don't we just take a break for a little while until I can sort out my feelings, if that's OK with you?"

Stuart just looked at her, then got up slowly and walked over to the window. Pretending he was looking out, he turned and said, "I love you, Babe, I'm not sure how else I can show you." Stuart said as he walked behind Martha, putting his hands on her shoulders. "This isn't a marriage proposal, just a weekend getaway to Vegas; but if this is what you want, then I will step back and give you some time. However, I would like to know in a couple of days, just so I can make the needed travel arrangements."

"Sure," Martha smiled, "I will let you know as soon as I do."

With that he strode out the door and down the hall to his office. Martha breathed a sigh of relief and felt some of the tension leave her body.

Chapter 23

Everyone was surprised to see Trent as he came in at the last minute to the meeting. "Hey Son," Henry said, as he got up to shake his hand.

"Hi. everyone," Trent said, as he looked around and smiled.

Terry noticed dark circles around his eyes. "Let me get you a cup of coffee," she said, as she got up to make a fresh pot.

"Thanks", Trent said, and sat down near Martha. Martha smiled and grabbed his hand and squeezed him hard. Taking the cup of coffee from Terry, he gulped it down and bit into a pastry as if he hadn't eaten in days.

"Wow, you must be hungry," Martha laughed.

"I didn't eat yesterday, so guess I am," he replied quietly.

"I see," Martha said, and looked over towards Henry, who was nodding sympathetically.

"Oh, Trent! It's so good to see you here," Claire said as she came in. I wasn't sure you would be able to come today."

"Thanks, I just felt like getting out of the house. Thought I would try to go over to the church and see how far I'm behind on my work as well!"

"Well, if you need me to keep little Jacob, just let me know," Claire responded.

"That goes for me too," Terry chimed in!

Trent laughed, "Well, let me put you on the waiting list then. It seems everyone wants little Jacob!"

"I bet so," Henry said. "He's such a good little boy."

"That he is," Trent grinned. "He's sure kept his dad sane lately!"

"Well, as you all know," Claire said looking at everyone, this is the 4th week you've been meeting, and next week Mr. Williams will be coming back to speak with you about your challenges. I'm not sure where each of you is in getting these accomplished, but I urge you to complete them as soon as possible."

Martha looked down at her hands and noticed that she was wringing them, hoping no one would ask her about what she had done.

It was then that Terry spoke up and told everyone that she would be seeing her Mom that weekend. Henry also said that he was in the process of planning a trip to see each of his kids and he would appreciate them praying for him.

"Well," Trent looked around. "I did approach my Senior Pastor several weeks ago about a possible sabbatical, and the board was going to meet this week to discuss and vote on it. Then Maggie's accident happened, so I suppose everything is on hold now. Frankly, I don't see it happening at all. Because of my circumstances, I think I should just bow out of the group."

"No," Claire spoke first. "Absolutely not!"

"I second that," Terry said, and the others agreed. "Why don't we pray about it?" Henry added. "Let's just see what the Lord will do?"

"Well, OK, I guess it can't hurt," Trent smiled sadly. As they all grabbed hands Henry led them in a quick prayer.

Afterwards Martha stood up and said she needed to be excused for a moment. They all looked at each other and noticed tears in her eyes as she walked out of the room.

"I wonder what that was that all about," Terry said quietly.

"Maybe she's struggling with her challenge," Trent commented. "I seem to remember it's about forgiving her ex-husband."

"Oh, that's right," Terry nodded. "Guess I should go see how she's doing?"

"I would," Henry smiled, and reached over to pat her hand.

Trent smiled and was so glad that he had this group to talk to. He realized that as a minister he really had no one to vent or share his grief with. "Henry, do you have plans after the meeting today?" Trent suddenly asked.

"No just planning on going home to start packing for my trip."

"Would you mind if we grabbed a quick bite to eat?"

"I would like that," Henry smiled.

"Thanks," Trent said, and then noticed the ladies coming back into the room.

"I'm so sorry for interrupting the meeting like that," Martha said as she sat down. "But I've been struggling lately", and then the tears started falling again. They all waited until she could talk and noticed Terry had taken her hand.

"Anyway, when I got my challenge, it was to forgive my husband, as you all know. I just couldn't, because it hurt too bad. However, through some bad choices of my own lately, I see how an affair can start. It's almost like skiing down a mountainside. You start off slow, then all of a sudden, you're going faster and faster, and can't seem to stop. So, now I can see how my husband could have done this. In fact, I also realize how I drove him to do it with my critical attitude. So, if you all could pray for me, that I would be able to speak to him, and perhaps have some sort of reconciliation, I would appreciate it."

"Sure, why don't we pray now," Trent said, as he grabbed her hand. So, they all bowed their heads again and prayed that the Lord would move in Martha's life.

Claire walked beside the open door and listened in as the group huddled around each other. Smiling, she silently thanked God for the unity this group finally had, even with its rocky start. After the meeting, Henry walked into her office. Standing there, watching her on the phone, he thought to himself she sure is an attractive woman. Claire looked up and saw him staring at her. Smiling, she held up her hand indicating for him to wait. He nodded and turned around to see Trent standing near the elevator. "Can you wait just a second, Trent? I need to ask Claire a question before we go?"

"Sure, I need to call the office anyway."

Henry smiled and turned back around to see that Claire was up and walking towards him.

"So how do you think the meeting went today?" she asked.

"Well, I think it was really the first time people let their guards down and were honest with each other."

"Yes, I sensed that too. I have to admit I was skeptical at first. I just wasn't sure this group was going to gel."

"Well, it takes time for people to open up. In fact, that's why I'm here."

"Really?" Claire replied. "So, what's going on, Henry?"

"Well, as you know, I'm going to see each of my children and get some things resolved. And I was thinking that if you had some time off, you might want to come with me?"

Surprised, she leaned back on her desk, and looked into his eyes. Henry just smiled at her and continued. "Well, I thought we had something growing between us, and that you needed to know more about me and my family."

"Oh, I see," Claire smiled.

"Well, let me see what I can do about taking some vacation days. By the way, how long might this trip take?"

Well, I've got three children that live all over the country, so maybe two weeks? In fact, we will be staying with friends and family most of the time if that's not too uncomfortable for you."

"That would be great. I would love to go. Just let me check with my boss, and I will let you know by the end of the day."

"Good, good," Henry said, as he hugged her good bye. "Well I need to go. Trent and I are having lunch together."

"Oh, that's nice. You two have a good time."

"Thanks, I think it will be good to just listen and be there for him."

"Yes, he needs that being a minister. I'm sure they don't have the support that's really needed in their position."

"True. I will call you this evening, if that's all right?"

"Yes, looking forward to it. And Henry, thanks for thinking about me and inviting me on your trip!"

"You're very welcome!" As he walked away, he sighed and said, *thank you Lord!*

Chapter 24

Henry squeezed the lemon into his tea, and looked at Trent, "So how are you really doing son?"

"To tell you the truth, I'm struggling, Henry. I was already stressed before the accident, and quite frankly I'm not sure that I can continue going at this pace. Being a single dad right now, without Maggie, is a little overwhelming."

"I can only imagine," Henry looked down at the plate of food the waitress had put in front of him. "Wow, they sure do give big portions, don't they?"

Trent smiled and played around with his salad.

"Is that all you're eating?" Henry asked as he munched on his hamburger.

"Yes, I've not been too hungry lately, but I needed to lose some weight anyway!"

"Well, not this way," Henry said, in his fatherly manner. "So, what can I do to help? I know I will be gone for a couple of weeks, but I sure would love to help in some way."

"Well, to tell you the truth, I've needed someone to just talk to. Maybe we can meet once a week for breakfast or something if that's OK?"

"Of course," Henry smiled, "I would love to do that! And even when I'm away, we can talk by phone. So, have you thought about getting some help once Maggie comes home?"

"That's if she comes home," Trent interrupted.

"Oh, ye of little faith," Henry grinned. "Of course, she will. It may take some time, but I have full confidence in the Lord that He spared her for a reason, and still has a plan for her life! A life that includes you and your little boy."

"You see, that's why I need to talk to you every week," Trent chuckled. "I need someone to lean on when my faith is weak!"

"Good, I'm glad I can help." Now as I said don't you think you should line up some help once Maggie comes home?"

"Yes, I guess I should be looking. I will get on that today!" Henry took another big bite of his hamburger, "This is good," he said, as he wiped his mouth.

Trent just smiled and thought, what a gift this inheritance group had been after all. Forget the money, the friendships that the Lord has given me are priceless.

Terry walked into her apartment. As she threw her pocketbook down on the couch she noticed her wedding invitation on her coffee table. "Oh no! I totally forgot I have a wedding shower this weekend!" Her cell phone vibrated in her purse. Picking it up she saw it was Jeffery. "Hi honey," she said wearily.

"Hey beautiful! You sound tired. What's going on?"

Unforeseen

"Oh, I planned on seeing my mom this weekend, and I just remembered the wedding shower we have."

"Well, that's why I'm calling. I'm working on a case, and it looks like I'm going to have to be at the office all day Saturday. So, I was wondering if I can just meet you there?"

"Well, just make sure you show up," Terry said, a little annoyed.

"I will," Jeffery replied. "I'm sure it's going to be fun."

"Yes, I'm sure it is," Terry said, not so enthusiastically.

"Are you OK?" Jeffery asked, "We haven't seen each other in a while, and I feel like you've been avoiding me."

"No Honey. Like I said, there's a lot going on right now."

"So, why don't we at least go for coffee in the morning, before the weekend begins?" he said.

"Sure, that sounds good," Terry replied. "In fact, I know a cute little diner that's close to both of us. Why don't we meet there?"

"Sounds like a plan," Jeffery said. "Well good night Baby!"

"Good night Honey." Terry then looked around at all her unopened mail, checked her doors, and headed straight to bed.

Trent reached in his pocket to get his keys and sighed as he began the drive to the hospital. He could almost do it blindfolded by now. He wished it were just a bad dream he could wake up from. Suddenly his phone rang, and he saw that it was his boss. "Hello, Trent," Pastor Jim said loudly.

"Hi, Pastor," Trent replied. Is something wrong?"

"No, just checking to see about the youth service on Sunday. Is everything in place?"

"As far as I know," Trent replied. "I've still got to get someone to help set up the fellowship hall for lunch that day, but I've got one of the women's classes doing the cooking, so I will check again with Gloria."

"Great! I've got the order of service ready to be turned in this morning, and I wanted to go over it with you quickly when you come in. You are coming in today, aren't you?"

"Yes, I just wanted to run by the hospital to see Maggie first, if that's OK with you?"

"Sure, I have a lunch appointment at 1:00pm, so hopefully we can connect before I leave."

"I'll stop by your office as soon as I get there, Sir."

"Trent, know that I am praying for you during this time."

"Thanks," Trent said, "I appreciate it."

Trent put his phone away and headed into the hospital corridor. He stepped into the elevator and closed his eyes as it climbed slowly up to the floor that was becoming strangely too familiar by the day. As he approached his wife's room, he prayed for the strength to see her again. *If she would just wake up, perhaps they could have a conversation and share a laugh* together he thought.

Opening the door, he noticed Martha standing there, holding his wife's hand, tears streaming down her face. "Martha," Trent spoke softly. "Are you all right?"

Startled, she looked up and said nothing. Trent came in, moving closer to her.

"I'm sorry," Martha said, backing away. "I shouldn't be here, but I just had you and your wife on my mind when I woke up this morning. I just felt like I needed to come over. I hope I'm not intruding?"

"No, not at all. I'm just surprised to see you."

Unforeseen

"I know," Martha smiled. "I'm sure I've been pretty insensitive in the meetings, and I don't share your views on spirituality. But know that I do care, and I've been praying for you all, too."

"Well, we appreciate it for sure," Trent smiled. "I know the Lord is hearing all the prayers."

"Well I can't say that I know that for sure," Martha said quickly. "But if there's someone out there, then hopefully he is hearing us."

"Can I buy you a cup of coffee?" Martha asked as she grabbed her pocketbook.

"Thanks for the offer," Trent said. "But I can't stay long today I've got to get to work myself. Oh, and thank you, for coming!"

"You're welcome. If there's anything I can do, please let me know."

"Thanks, I guess I will see you next Thursday morning," Trent added.

"Yeah, I guess I'll be there. Not sure why I keep coming though," Martha said as she laughed.

"Well, who knows what will come of it. But I do know that I'm glad I met you all, especially since this happened." Trent said.

"Yes, I guess you could say we are at least becoming friends, aren't we?" Martha said after she thought a minute."

"Absolutely," Trent added, "Nothing is an accident with God."

"Really?" Martha looked at Trent.

"Sure," Trent said.

"Well, I don't have time to debate that statement, but perhaps we can talk more about it next week," Martha smiled.

"That would be great," he said, as he walked her to the elevator.

"Well, like I said before, if I can do anything else to help you, just let me know," Martha repeated as the door opened.

"Thanks again," Trent smiled, and turned back to the room. Noticing a doctor and nurse rushing into his wife's room, he walked quickly back down the hall.

Unforeseen

Chapter 25

Henry finished packing and took his cup of coffee and stepped out onto the porch. He couldn't contain the excitement that was building inside of him. Looking over at his neighbor's home, he thought about letting them know he would be gone for a couple of weeks just so they wouldn't be worried. But just then Stella came running over to him. "Hey there," Henry said smiling.

"Hey yourself," she grinned, and he noticed she was toothless.

"So, what happened to your two front teeth?"

"Oh, they just fell out, and I got a whole two dollars for them!" She reached into her pocket and pulled out the quarters!

"Well, now," Henry said. "Perhaps I should give you a quarter to go with those you already have?"

"Wow, I think that's a good idea," she grinned.

"Listen, Stella, is your dad or mom home?"

"My mom is, why?"

"Well, I just need to speak to her a minute. Let's walk over together," and he took her hand in his.

Calling Claire, Henry told her he was on his way, and would meet her at the front door of her apartment building. "I'm so excited," she said right before they hung up.

"Me too, Honey. So glad you're going with me. But let's pray my children feel the same way," Henry said.

"They will. I have been praying so much for this trip already. I just know the Lord is ordaining this at just the right time."

"I hope so," Henry remarked, "I certainly hope so."

Martha sat at her desk staring out the window, when suddenly Stuart leaned over and kissed her neck. Startled, she looked up, her head hitting him in the nose.

"What's wrong with you?" Stuart said, as he looked to see if he was bleeding.

"Nothing," she said defensively. "Sorry, but you should have warned me you were coming."

"Warned?" Stuart grimaced. "What am I, a nuclear weapon?"

With that Martha laughed, and went over to check the copy machine. "I didn't mean to hurt your feelings. I just have a lot on my mind today."

"It's that crazy inheritance group isn't it?" he smirked. "Ever since you started those weekly meetings, you've been preoccupied."

"You mean I haven't been with you every night," Martha said impatiently.

"No, I just mean you're not the same person. What's gotten into you?"

"Nothing," Martha said, and walked around him, pretending to shuffle her papers.

Stuart rubbed his chin. "You're not getting all spiritual on me, are you?"

"What?" Martha said exasperated. "Absolutely not!"

"Oh, I believe you are. You just don't want to admit it, even to yourself."

"I don't know what you are referring to, but I am the same person I've always been. Thank you very much." Martha turned around to the copy machine, her back towards Stuart.

"Well, you're not acting like it. If you are starting to feel like you are compromising being with me, then feel free to break up."

With that Martha just stopped and stared at him wide-eyed. "I see," she said slowly. "Just because I'm not at your beck and call, you have a temper tantrum."

"I don't know what you're talking about. I'm not a kid, and neither are you, I might add. We are both adults, and if you are starting to feel uncomfortable about our arrangement, then you can move out and get your own place."

"Oh, now the picture is becoming clearer by the minute. One thing you need to know Stuart, is that I can't be bought, and I don't need a free ride, certainly not from you."

"I'm not saying that Honey, I'm just stating a fact. Like I said, "I love you Martha, but I feel like you're not that crazy about me, and that hurts."

Stuart then heard a noise and turned towards the door. His wife was standing just inside the office, her face pale as a ghost. Seeing her, Stuart turned around and walked out the door. Martha just stood there for a minute digesting what had just happened. She realized she hadn't taken a breath and suddenly felt very light headed. Going towards her desk, she barely made it when everything went dark.

Trent entered the room and saw the doctor and nurse frantically working on Maggie.

"What's wrong?" Trent said loudly, and they both turned at the same time to look at him.

"Her vital signs plummeted, and we don't know what's going on. Please step out of the room," the doctor ordered.

Just then the crash cart came in, almost knocking him down. He rushed out into the hall and tried to catch his breath silently praying that God would intervene. Walking up and down the corridor, he kept watching for someone to come out and update him, but the minutes just ticked away.

Suddenly the doctor appeared He looked relieved.

"So, what's just happened?" Trent asked, wondering why he seemed so happy.

"Well, you won't believe it, but as we were working on her, her heart started beating normally, and her eyes begin to flutter. She woke up and started talking to us! It really is a miracle! I asked her some general questions, and she knew all the right answers."

Trent jumped up and down saying, "Isn't it about time you acknowledge that prayer really does change things?"

Laughing the doctor nodded and said "Yes, I suppose so. Anyway, she's asking for you."

Before the doctor could finish his sentence, Trent was running down the hall silently thanking the Lord. Opening the door, he saw Maggie look his way with that familiar smile on her face. Running towards her, he grabbed her hand and gave her the biggest kiss, right on the lips.

"Wow," she said. "I've missed those!" They both laughed and held each other a long time.

"Tell me, Honey, how long have I been in here?"

"Almost two weeks," Trent said. " It seems like a lifetime though. In fact, I was getting ready to leave for work when you stopped breathing."

"Yes, I seem to remember hearing some kind of music ... I thought I was dreaming. Then I woke up feeling like I was drowning ... and couldn't breathe. It scared me. That's then I heard all these voices calling my name."

"Wow," Trent said, "it sounds like you were dying."

"Yes, I think so, but the Lord has other things in mind for me."

"Yes," Trent agreed. "He knew Jacob and I needed you!"

Smiling Maggie took ahold of his hand, and they were one again. Trent prayed, and they each gave thanks to God for bringing them back together.

Chapter 26

Terry looked around for Jeffery, who was nowhere to be found. Disappointed she grabbed another glass of wine and strolled over to the snack table. Feeling a hand on her back, she looked around quickly to see her mom smiling.

"Hey Hon, thanks so much for inviting me to your shower."

"Well, Mom, that's the least I could do since I couldn't come to you. By the way, thanks for coming. I know it was a long drive."

"Not really, Marty drove me up. He was on his way to his daughter's. Which reminds me, I was wondering if you and Jeffery could have brunch with us tomorrow?"

"I don't see why not, that is unless he has to work, which is where he is today."

"Oh, I was wondering where he was hiding," her mom chuckled. "You know showers really aren't high on a man's priority list."

"Well, even if that's true," Terry smiled, "I'm still a little frustrated that he isn't here yet. We need to start opening the gifts together, and I hate making excuses for him."

"I understand," her mom replied, "but the big job and big pay always come with a big price."

Terry was about to respond when she saw Jeffery out of the corner of her eye. "Well speak of the devil," she said sarcastically. Waving he walked over stopping to speak to people as he passed by.

"Hello Beautiful," he said as he leaned down to kiss her on the cheek.

"Was just wondering if you would be here before we opened our gifts."

"Hello," Terry's mom spoke, as she reached out to shake his hand.

"Good afternoon, Mrs. Martin. I didn't know you would be here."

"Well, it was a last-minute invite. But I take what I can get when it comes to my daughter."

Terry bit her tongue and smiled ever so slightly towards Jeffery. Noticing the look, he quickly grabbed her and strolled off saying that they needed a little time together. Terry looked back and waved to her mom, who was standing there with her mouth wide open.

"Thanks for the quick escape Honey," Terry said as she grabbed his hand.

"At least I'm good for something," Jeffery winked.

"I wouldn't say that. You have a few more qualities I admire," she laughed.

"Well, that's a good thing, because I feel like I've been skating on thin ice for a while now."

"Why would you say that?" she looked into his eyes.

"I don't know," he said, as he grabbed a drink. "I just feel a distance every time we are together. Perhaps it's me," he continued, "and my busy schedule, or it's just the added stress of the wedding. Like I said the other night, we need to spend more time together."

"Well, at least we had coffee this morning," Terry interrupted, "that was nice, wasn't it?"

"Yes, but we need to do it at least once a week," Jeffery added.

"I agree," Terry said, just as he bent down to give her a kiss. "What was that for?" she smiled.

"Just because I love you!"

"Thanks," Terry said, as she leaned up against his shoulder. But secretly she wondered if her love was as strong as his seemed to be.

Terry and her mom got home late, and her mom headed for bed.

Fixing herself a cup of tea she sat down on the couch and closed her eyes tightly. *What an evening,* she thought. *Now, if I can just get through tomorrow's discussion with Mom, then perhaps my life can settle down a little... or maybe not* she frowned. *It all depends on her response* she thought, as she took another sip. Turning her thoughts to Jeffery, she still wondered, *if marrying him was the right thing to do. I suppose this is what all my friends describe as "cold feet."*

Shaking her head, she got up and looked out the kitchen window, and felt a sinking feeling that she just might be settling... and she didn't want that for her, or for Jeffery.

"Honey?" Startled, Terry looked around to see her mom standing behind her, in her robe and slippers.

"What is it, Mom?"

"Oh, I wanted to wash my face, but I can't seem to find the washcloths."

"That's because I forgot to lay them out for you," Terry smiled.

As she turned around she noticed tears in her mom's eyes." Are you all right?" Terry stopped and put her hand on her Mom's arm.

"Yes, I was just thinking about when you were little, and now how beautiful and mature you've become. I'm just so glad you're my daughter," she said, as she hugged Terry's neck.

Taken back she looked into her mom's eyes, and she saw a sincerity and love she had never seen before. "Wow, you surprise me," Terry responded, as she reached into the closet to grab some towels and washcloths to give her mom.

"I know, I've not been the most lovable mother to you. For that I am sorry."

"You're right about that," Terry said, a little short.

"But," her mom continued, "I just want you to know that I do love you despite my past actions."

"Why don't we continue this conversation tomorrow, Mom? We're both tired tonight, and I've had a very long day and need to get some sleep."

"I'm sorry, I didn't mean to open a can of worms right at bedtime."

"That's OK, I've just had a busy week, and tons to do. If you need anything else, just knock on my door."

"OK, honey. Sleep well."

"You too. Oh, and there is plenty of food in the fridge, and the coffee pot is already set to just turn on in the morning, in case you get up before me, which is highly probable."

Laughing, her mom hugged her again and said "Thanks."

Looking at her mom walk down the hall Terry wondered *what in the world had gotten into her? She was acting so different. Well, maybe the conversation tomorrow will go better than expected. One can only hope* she thought, as she turned towards her bedroom for the night.

Chapter 27

Martha looked around her apartment, making note of all the boxes yet to pack. Well, she thought, *it was nice while it lasted.* But deep down she knew she never really had peace playing the role of mistress. Despite losing her job, and her dwelling, something inside of her was excited. It didn't make any sense, but neither did much in her life right now.

Terry had been kind enough to let her crash at her place for a while, so at least she wouldn't be homeless! She glanced at her watch, and realized she needed to leave for the inheritance meeting. Never one to open up about her life personally, she was ready to share with them what had happened and to finally be honest, for once in her life. Hearing her phone, she reached into her purse and answered it, before she looked to see who it was. "Hello," she said mindlessly.

"Hey there," Stuart said a little timidly.

"Yes?" Martha said a little too short.

"Thought I would check up on you to see how you've been?"

"I'm fine Stuart, how can I help you?"

Stuart was silent for a minute. "I just wanted to apologize for the way I acted the other day. I know I said some pretty nasty things to you, but I was just hurt that you didn't want to come with me to Las Vegas. I still love you, Martha, and I want us to be together."

Martha was quiet for a minute. "Stuart, I'm glad it happened, really. It gave me a chance to evaluate where I am in my life. I've been uncomfortable playing the 'mistress card', so I think it's worked out for both of us, really. Oh, just so you know, I'll be moving out of the apartment on Friday, and it will be vacant for whoever is next for you."

"Oh, that's rich," Stuart said impatiently. "I don't have women waiting in the wings, if that's what you're referring too. I told you, you could stay as long as you needed. And by the way, I would love to have you back working for me."

"No, I don't think that's wise. I'm packed, and I already have a place to stay. I'm sure I'll have a job soon enough. Listen, I've got to go," she said as she glanced at her watch, "I have a meeting at 9am."

"Oh, yes. Let me guess. It's that crazy inheritance thing, isn't it?" he laughed.

Biting her tongue, she didn't respond. "Good-bye Stuart, and I really hope you have a nice life, OK?"

He was silent for a moment. "Sure, I always have, haven't I?" and he quickly hung up.

"Oh brother," Martha said out loud, "like I needed that this morning."

♦ ♦ ♦

Trent and Terry arrived early, grabbing a cup of coffee. Martha came running in out of breath. "So sorry," she smiled. "I had a phone call that made me late."

"Oh, that's OK," Terry grinned. "We just got here ourselves, and Henry isn't here this week. He and Claire are on a trip together."

"Oh really?" Martha said smiling. "Seems like they're quite an item now."

Trent laughed and said, "Well love grows in all seasons."

"Sure does," Terry said thoughtfully. "By the way, how is Maggie doing?"

Trent smiled, "I wanted to wait until everyone was here to tell you the good news."

As he began describing what had happened that morning after Martha came by, they all were amazed at the healing God was giving Maggie. "So," Martha interrupted. "will she be able to come home soon?"

"Well, right now they're planning to send her to the rehab hospital for physical therapy."

"That's wonderful!" Terry smiled. "Looks like your God has heard all the prayers, hasn't He?"

Trent looked at her and nodded, "Yes, He sure has."

Martha looked at Terry and said, "Are you getting all spiritual now too?"

Laughing, Terry said, "I'm not really sure where that last statement came from," shaking her head, "but maybe I am starting to question if there is a God."

Trent seized the moment to speak to them about faith and God's love for them.

Martha sat quietly and pondered this new concept. "Well I know I've got a conscience that knows right from wrong, because

I've just gotten out of a situation at work that wasn't right. In fact, Terry knows this, she's letting me stay at her house until I get back on my feet."

"Really?" Trent replied.

Martha couldn't hold it in any longer. She looked down and started to cry. Then everything she had in her head came tumbling out of her mouth. Terry grabbed a tissue handing it to her, and Trent got up and knelt down at her feet.

"Listen, Martha, we've all missed the mark somewhere in our lives. We're not perfect, God knows this. That's why He came to die for us. He knew we were lost and needed to be shown the right way back home. Eventually, we all come to a crossroad in our lives where we have to choose to either go our own way or go God's. Are you ready to do it God's way?"

Suddenly every thought, every action that she had done since age five came rushing back to her. She felt like she was looking at a movie of her life—all the bad choices she had made, and the many times she shook her fist at God. Breathing deeply, she nodded, Yes, and again sobbed.

As Trent led her in a prayer, she felt a weight being lifted off her chest, and a deep sense of joy she had never experienced. Suddenly her sobbing turned into laugher, and she smiled for the first time in a long time. Trent smiled too, then hugged her.

Terry just sat there, not knowing what to do. Tears were rolling down her cheeks as well, but suddenly she felt like an outsider listening in to a private conversation, which didn't include her. Trent turned around to Terry. "How are you doing?"

"Feeling a little awkward," she said quietly.

"There's no need for that," Trent smiled. "You just said yourself that you were thinking more about spiritual things. Are you ready to make a decision to trust God as well?"

"I'm not sure. I'm still dealing with a lot of hurts, and I haven't even talked to my mom yet. She came this weekend, but something about the way she was acting made me uncomfortable bringing up the past. I guess I chickened out."

"That's OK. God knows the right time. Perhaps He was telling you to wait until your mom is ready to listen."

"Perhaps, but I need to get this behind me before the wedding."

"Maybe not," Trent said. "Maybe there's some things you need to resolve before you deal with this?"

"Never thought of it that way," Terry said thoughtfully. "Anyway, I'm happy for you Martha, I really am. But I don't think it's for me, not yet anyway."

"That's OK," Martha said quietly and turned to Trent, who also nodded.

"Don't do anything you don't want to," he responded.

With that they continued the meeting and decided next week to meet at the diner up the street, if the lawyer would agree to it. As they were leaving, Martha looked around the room and everything seemed so different looking. She couldn't explain how she felt … but for the first time in her life, she felt loved … and that felt good, really good!

Chapter 28

Henry and Claire pulled into the hotel, got out and stretched their legs. "I tell you, traveling isn't for the faint hearted is it?" Henry said laughing.

"No, it isn't," Claire chuckled. "But it is fun to explore and see new things."

"Well, I say we get our rooms, then go out for a nice dinner," Henry looked Claire's way.

"That sounds nice," Claire smiled. "I would like to freshen up a bit before we eat."

"Great idea," Henry said, as he lifted the trunk to get their luggage; that way I can call my daughter and let her know we are close."

As they went into the lobby she spotted a coffee pot. "Oh, I think I will get me a cup of coffee while you check us in."

"OK," he said, as he strolled up to the desk, and asked for two rooms.

The attendant looked surprised, but gave him two keys, and grinned. As Henry waited for the elevator, he heard his phone vibrating in his shirt pocket. Pulling it out, he saw it was his daughter. "Hey Honey," he said a little too loud. "We are just getting settled into the hotel, was going to call you!"

"Well, dad, I just wanted to say, I've got an out of town meeting tomorrow. So, it looks like I'm not going to be able to meet you two for dinner tomorrow evening after all."

Feeling disappointed, Henry replied, "I see, is there another time we could meet you then?"

"Well, I'm not sure," she hesitated. "Why is it that you're here?"

Taken back by her abruptness, he didn't know how to respond.

"Dad, are you there?"

"Yes, Honey, I just wanted to be able to see you and spend a little time catching up."

"Well, if I get home in time, perhaps we can meet for coffee and dessert?"

"That's fine, Sweetheart, whatever you can do would be great."

"OK, I will call you tomorrow?" she said, hanging up quickly.

Feeling a little dejected, he stuck his phone back into this pocket and headed up to his room.

Terry called her counselor to see if they could meet.

"Sure," Ron said, as he checked his calendar. "I think I have time to see you at 3:00pm today, if that works?"

"Yes, that would be perfect," Terry said, and quickly made a note for herself. "Thanks, Ron!"

"No problem. Is everything OK?"

"Yes, just something I want to bounce off you."

"I understand. See you this afternoon then."

Unforeseen

As the afternoon progressed Terry kept finding herself thinking back to the prayer Martha prayed and to the things Trent had said about God. Restless, she told her secretary she was going out for a cup of coffee.

As she walked along the river's edge, she found herself praying, "Lord, if you are real, then please show yourself to me. I need to know if you really love me, or was I a big mistake after all?"

Suddenly, she saw a dove fly near and land on the sidewalk right in front of her. "Well, aren't you beautiful?" Terry said as she reached out to pet it. Suddenly the little bird jumped onto her arm and just sat there, for a moment. Then the bird chirped, and off it went, as quickly as it'd come.

Well, that was strange she said silently, but she also felt a bit of excitement that it had happened right after she'd prayed. *I wonder if this was a coincidence or maybe there is a God trying to let me know He cares and was listening to me!*

As Henry and Claire headed out to see his daughter the following evening, Claire looked over at him. "Are you nervous?" she asked.

"A little," he turned and smiled. "I was hoping we would have a little more time together, but she's always been one to avoid anything too uncomfortable."

"I see," Claire said. "Perhaps this little bit of time then will break the ice between you two."

"I hope so, I've been praying a long time for my children; at least this is a start. I've been feeling for a while that I needed to do more to reach out. So, hopefully this will show them I'm trying."

"Yes," Claire nodded. "I think it's going to show them that you want to establish a better relationship."

"Just so you know," Henry looked Claire's way. "Marisa is an independent business woman, and quite wealthy. In fact, she acts a lot like I did at her age."

"Like the ole saying, 'like father, like daughter' uh," Claire winked?

"Yes, you could say that, but not in a good way, I'm afraid," Henry frowned.

"I don't agree," Claire said. "I think she's probably got some of your good qualities too, in fact I'm banking on that."

"Well, that would be a nice surprise," Henry looked over at Claire. "Looks like we have arrived," he said, as they pulled into a swanky coffee shop that protruded out towards Lake Michigan.

"What a beautiful view," Claire commented, as she got out of the car.

"Sure is," Henry responded as he looked around. Just then, he saw Marisa waving at him from her car.

Waving back, he motioned for Claire to come around, so he could take her hand.

"Well look who has grown up," Henry smiled, as he hugged Marisa tightly.

"Looks like we've all gotten a little older, haven't we?" Marisa said, as she looked at her Dad closely. "And who is this?" she glanced over to Claire.

"Why, hello," Claire said and then hugged Marisa, before she realized what was going on. "I'm a friend of your Dad, I hope you don't mind me being here!"

"No, not at all," Marisa said. "In fact, I also brought my fiancé. He's already inside getting us a table. As you can see this cafe is really popular because of the lakefront view it has."

"Yes, I was admiring how lovely it is," Claire replied as she looked around.

"So, I guess we should go on inside," Henry said as he opened the door for the ladies. As Claire passed by, she touched his hand lightly, and smiled. Nodding at her, he winked and took a deep breath, dreading the next hour.

Chapter 29

Terry knocked on Ron's door lightly and heard a faint "Come in."

"Hello?" Terry said, as she stepped through the door. Not seeing anyone, she sat down in her familiar chair. Ron came out of another room with a cup of coffee in his hand.

"Would you like a cup?" he said smiling.

"No, thank you," Terry nodded, "I just had lunch before I came over."

"So, tell me what's going on with you?"

"Well, for starters my mom came down last weekend for a wedding shower I had, and she stayed over at my house."

"Were you able to speak to her?" Ron asked.

"No, it was late when we came in, and there was something about her that was so different, I couldn't put my finger on it. So, guess I chickened out."

Laughing, Ron leaned back and replied, "Don't beat yourself up. Timing is everything. Just wait on the Lord, and He will direct you."

Unforeseen

"Speaking of the Lord," Terry said, "In our inheritance group there is a lady who at first was pretty rude and an atheist. She wasn't interested in spiritual things at all. But yesterday, she did something really crazy."

"What happened?" Ron leaned in towards Terry.

"Well, Trent started praying with her about some issues she was having, and, well, she did something I don't really understand."

"What did she do?" Ron smiled.

"She ended up praying some kind of prayer asking Jesus to come into her heart!"

"Really!" Ron smiled. "That's great!

"But how can someone who's so against a 'higher power' suddenly change like that? I mean, that's crazy don't you think?" Terry said frowning. "I admit I'm searching, and I think I'm spiritual and all that, but please."

Ron just sat there praying and asking the Lord for the right words.

Terry continued on. "Something strange did happen to me this morning as I went to get coffee before work. I was walking, and I started to ask God to show to me if He was real. Then suddenly a dove appeared right in front of me, and as I bent down he flew up on my arm. He let me touch him, then quickly flew away!"

"Interesting," Ron said. Waiting a few seconds, he began sharing his own testimony of how the Lord delivered him from drugs and alcohol and then led him down a road of helping others with similar problems. That is when I felt a calling to go into full-time ministry and counseling. So here I am, twenty years later." he smiled.

As Terry just sat there, quietly listening, she noticed how sincere he was.

"Oh, I'm sorry," Ron said. "Sometimes I get too long-winded."

"No not at all. I was just thinking about how sincere you are. Your story is really interesting, but I'm just not sure I can trust someone who I can't see, and who supposedly made all this, and ..." She threw her hands up to the ceiling. "I mean, can you blame me? Look at this mess the world is in."

Ron was quiet for a minute. Terry got up from her chair and began to pace back and forth. "Besides, Jeffery is an avowed agnostic, and he wants nothing to do with religion or the church, though he does admit there's something bigger out there."

Ron sat back in his chair and rubbed his face for a moment. "Let me ask you something. Do you think you are here for a reason, a purpose?"

Terry thought for a moment. "I think so, or else the abortion would have worked, right? I mean, there's some reason why I survived."

"That's right," Ron said thoughtfully. "So, if there is a reason you're here, then wouldn't it be possible that the One Who created you, would have a plan for your life?"

"I guess," Terry nodded.

"So," Ron continued, "if He has a plan, then wouldn't you think part of that plan would be to have a relationship with you? Because to know the plan, you've got to know the one who formed it, right?"

"It makes sense," Terry said quietly.

"So, why not step out in faith and find out? I mean, what's it going to hurt? If I'm wrong, then you haven't lost anything. But if I'm right, you've gained everything."

Terry just sat there pondering it all, her head spinning.

Unforeseen

Trent rode up on the elevator towards his wife's room, with a smile on his face. Overjoyed at Martha's decision for Christ, and how she had changed over the last few weeks. He couldn't wait to tell Maggie what had happened. He walked into her room and saw her sitting up and reading her Bible.

"Well, hey Beautiful," he said, as he kissed her cheek. "Don't you look chipper this morning?"

"Well, thank you," she looked up smiling. "It's the first time I've felt like sitting up. I can't wait for my strength to come back."

"I'm sure it won't be long now," Trent said, as he sat down next to her. "So, what are you reading?" he asked looking over her shoulder.

"Oh, the Psalms," she glanced up at him. "I'm finding myself just thanking and praising the Lord for all He has done for me!"

"We do have so much to thank Him for, don't we?" he hugged her gently.

"I've been thinking," Maggie said carefully, "when I come home it might be wise if we had someone to help me out. At least until I can get my strength back and can do things on my own again."

"Yes, I suppose so. But I'm a pretty good assistant, aren't I?" Trent said, laughing.

"Of course, Honey, but you've got a job, and you've missed enough work already,"

"Well, let's pray about it and see who comes to mind," Trent replied.

"Well," Maggie said slowly. "I think I know who it should be. I've also been praying for a few days, and I believe the Lord put Martha on my mind."

Trent just looked at her with his mouth wide opened. "Why would you think of her?"

"I'm not sure. I know she came by several times to see me. She would introduce herself and just start talking. I couldn't process everything she said, but I could tell she was a nice lady."

"Well, you won't believe what happened in the meeting this morning," and he began telling Maggie everything.

"Amazing, so I guess I did hear the Lord right. I think we should ask her if she might be at least open to the idea?"

"OK," Trent agreed. Just then the doctor came in and started checking her vitals.

"Well," he looked up smiling. "You're doing great, Maggie. Your mind is alert, and your memory is excellent. However, your body needs to catch up. I think we're going to move you to the rehab hospital a few miles down the road. After you've had some physical therapy, then we'll see when you can be discharged!"

"Sounds great," the couple said together, looking at each other, smiling.

"I'll get the paperwork started, and you two can start enjoying one another again. One thing though," he said as he turned to look at Trent, "you might want to think about hiring some help when you first get home."

Trent smiled, "Well, I believe Maggie has someone already in mind!"

"That's great, is it a nurse or friend?"

"Well, she's an acquaintance, but I believe she will work out well."

"Good. Just so you know, it will probably need to be twenty four-hour help at the beginning. Then as you get stronger, you can slowly decrease her hours."

"Sure," they both said, holding hands. "The Lord will provide."

"Well, if you're worried about money, your insurance should be able to help for the first few months anyway."

A look of relief came over both of them. "We certainly appreciate all you've done for us during this time, Doc."

"My pleasure," he smiled, "but I can't take all the credit. I'm just a tool in the Lord's hands."

"That's true," Trent spoke up, "I'm glad you acknowledge that."

"Always have and always will," he said, as he started out the door. Then looking at Maggie he said, "I believe the Lord has something else for you to do, or you wouldn't be here, Maggie. So while you're recuperating, you should ask Him what that might be."

Maggie looked at Trent with a surprised look and nodded.

Chapter 30

Feeling a little awkward, Henry and Claire sat down across from Marisa and her fiancé, Mark. But as soon as they started to talk things got a little easier. "So how did you two meet?" Marisa asked Claire, as she took a sip of her cappuccino.

"Well, it's kind of a long story, but I work for a law firm that distributes inheritances to people. Your father is a recipient of one, right now."

"Interesting," Marisa's fiancé interjected. "So, Henry, how much cash are you getting?" Mark asked.

Henry coughed, then looked up from eating and said, "Don't know yet," they aren't telling us until after the six weeks are up."

"Really?" Marisa commented. "That seems very odd to me. Are you sure it's legitimate? I mean, no offense to you, Claire, but it seems a little shady."

Smiling, Claire said, "Yes, it's legitimate, but it's more than just the money."

"Oh yeah?" Marisa's fiancé replied, "So what is it?"

"Well I really can't divulge the things we talk about. There are other's involved and they each have individual stipulations.

"Um," they both said, looking at each other.

"So, Dad, it seems you really haven't changed after all, have you?"

Henry looked up to see her smiling smugly at him.

"What are you talking about, Honey?"

"Well, you were always looking for a way to get a fast buck, so I guess this is just another one of those ways. Am I right?"

Henry put down his fork and sat there for a minute. Praying silently, he said "No, Honey, you aren't. In fact, you couldn't be more wrong." Looking into her eyes, Henry began sharing his newfound faith with her. As he confessed his sins against her, she began squirming in her seat.

"Well, I'm not sure I can handle any more of this 'Dr Phil' moment, but if that makes you happy, then I'm happy for you," Marisa continued, "however, if you think you're going to come in and suddenly be a dad to me, then you're sadly mistaken. I wrote you off a long time ago after Mom's death. Actually, I was hoping not to ever see you again."

Claire looked over to see if Henry was all right, but she was surprised to see a real peace despite the tear that rolled down his cheek.

"Honey, I understand. If I were in your shoes, I would probably be saying the same thing to me. But I want you to know that I miss your Mom every day. I hurt over my betrayal, not only to her, but to all three of you children. I was a lousy husband and father to you all. But I cannot change the past, what's done is done. But what I can do, is change the future, if you'll let me?"

Marisa looked down at her coffee, and then out the window to the beautiful lake and whispering clouds. Turning back to her father, she said, "I've got something to tell you."

"OK," Henry said as he leaned forward. "What is it Honey?"

"If you're on your way to see Sam after this, then you might as well head home."

"Why?" Henry asked as he glanced towards Claire.

"Because he's gone, Dad."

"Gone?" Henry said out loud. "What do you mean, is he out of the country?"

"No, he died last year in a crack house out in L.A."

Suddenly feeling dizzy, he put his hand on his forehead and begin shaking.

Claire took his arm, "Henry are you all right?"

All he was thinking was *I should have come sooner, I should have come sooner.* Just then a sharp pain hit him right in the center of his chest and he suddenly felt breathless. Grabbing his chest, he began to sweat profusely, and he looked at Claire.

"What is it Henry?" Claire reached for his hand.

"I think I'm having a heart attack," he said breathlessly.

His daughter grabbed her cell phone and quickly dialed 911. Suddenly Henry felt himself falling, and all he heard were muffled voices around him asking if he was all right.

The first thing Henry saw was Claire sitting beside him.

"Henry, you really scared us!"

"Where am I?" All he saw were machines hooked up to himself.

"You're in the hospital," Claire said. "You had a mild heart attack."

"Wow, bet you didn't plan on this, did you?" he said frowning.

"Oh, I plan for a lot of things, but one of them is not losing you. At least not for a long time," Claire said, taking hold of his hand.

"Where's Marisa?" he said as he looked out the door into the hallway.

"She and her fiancé were here for a long time but had to leave. She told me to tell you she would be back this evening after work. Oh, and there will be some sort of surprise too!"

"Well, I think she surprised me enough," he frowned, "but I wonder what she's up to now" he commented. She always loved surprises. I remember coming home from business trips and bringing the kids a little something each time. She would run up to me, hold out her hand, and beg for it before I could get in the door!"

"Well, maybe it's your turn to hold out your hand," Henry.

"Maybe so," Henry thought for a moment. Just then the door opened, and the doctor and nurse walked in.

"So, how's the patient doing this morning?" he grinned.

"I'm doing great," Henry said, as he sat up. "When can I leave?"

"Oh, you are already wanting to leave this wonderful place?" the doctor said, laughing as he looked down on his chart. "Let's give it another day and if all goes well, then you can be on your way, how's that?"

"Well, if you insist," Henry said, as he looked over at Claire. This pretty lady here has been left to fend on her own, and I promised her an adventure!"

"Well, I do believe you're giving her an adventure, just a different one," the doctor said and smiled. "If everything goes well today, I promise I will put discharge orders on your chart this evening, how's that?"

"Perfect," Henry said, and reached out to shake his hand.

As the doctor and nurse left, he turned around, and said to Claire, "Now let him rest, and you go get yourself something to eat," as he winked.

"Sure," Claire said squeezing Henry's hand.

Unforeseen

Chapter 31

Martha sipped her coffee and looked through the job listings. "So much for finding a job easily," she mumbled. "What?" Terry said, as she came into the kitchen.

"You're up early," Martha looked up from her computer.

"Yes, unfortunately I have an early morning appointment," Terry yawned as she grabbed a coffee cup from the shelf. "So, are you having any luck with the job search?"

"Well, I have two interviews tomorrow, but I'm not sure if they're the right fit for me." Rubbing her head, Martha stared out the window. "I just feel that there is something else, something new I'm supposed to be doing, but I don't know what that is."

"Well," Terry said, as she sat down and munched on her toast, "maybe you should just spend the day praying, now that you know God," she grinned.

"That's a good idea," Martha said, "but you could know Him too, Terry."

Well, I suppose, but I'm not quite ready to give my life to someone I can't even see."

"I understand," Martha said thoughtfully, "I felt the same way all my life, but I can't even describe the peace I feel now, even with having no job or place to live!"

"Well, you can stay here as long as you like," Terry nodded, "so don't worry about that!"

"So, how's the wedding planning going?" Martha asked reluctantly.

"Funny you should ask. I didn't want to say anything, but I've called the wedding off. At least for now. Jeffery and I just don't see eye to eye about some things. He hasn't come out and said this, but I think he believes I'm weak since I'm going to a counselor. So, we agreed that this was the best thing for both of us."

"Oh, I'm sorry," Martha reached over and touched Terry's hand.

"I'm not. I've been feeling restless long before this. So, hey maybe a higher power is protecting me," she laughed. "I know you would say it's Jesus, but I'm not going to go that far yet."

"Well, you're a beautiful woman, Terry, with a lot to offer someone. So just wait on God to show you."

Suddenly Martha's cell phone rang, and she quickly grabbed it out if her pocketbook.

"Hello? Martha, this is Trent. How are you doing?"

"Great. Is Maggie OK?"

"Oh, she's doing well. In fact, that's why I called. We were wondering if you had time today to meet us at the hospital? We both want to speak to you about something."

"Sure," Martha said, "What time are you thinking?"

"Well, I'm on my way to work right now, so how about noon, if that's OK with you?"

"I was going to the park today, so I'll come on over around lunch time."

"Great, thanks a lot. We look forward to seeing you!" As Martha put down the phone she had an odd sense of anticipation.

Unforeseen

"What was that about?" Terry said as she got up to grab her coat.

"That was Trent asking if I could meet them at the hospital around noon today."

"Really? Interesting. Well you need to tell me all about it when I get home this evening!"

"Oh, by the way, tomorrow is Wednesday, and that's our fifth meeting. Only one more to go," Terry said, as she headed out the door.

"That's right, and that lawyer said he would be there. Didn't he?' Martha replied.

"Yes, perhaps he'll finally tell us about our inheritance."

"I hope so," Martha said. "That money would sure come in handy right now."

"I know what you mean," Terry grinned. "See you later, and tell Trent and Maggie 'Hello', for me!"

"Sure will," Martha said, as she clicked on her computer again.

Martha walked into the hospital corridor and glanced around for Trent. I suppose he's already in with Maggie. Walking into the elevator she hardly noticed when a man stepped in right after her. "Martha is that you?"

Looking up she saw her ex-husband and gasped, "Frank, what in the world are you doing here?"

"My wife just had a baby girl, so I'm here to pick them up."

"Congratulations," Martha said feeling a little nauseous. "You must be overjoyed," she quipped.

Frank nodded. "I've always wanted children, as you well know."

"Well, excuse me, for robbing you of being a father. But I believe it was both our ideas not to have any children as they would get in the way of our lifestyle. Am I right?"

"Yes, you probably are," Frank frowned. "I guess we were both at fault then, weren't we?"

"I suppose." Martha frowned. "Listen Frank, I'm glad we bumped into one another. Do you have a minute to talk?"

"Well, I am in sort of a hurry, but why not."

As they both stepped off the elevator, they found a couple of chairs in the hall. Clearing her throat, Martha started telling him about her inheritance, and what had happened to her in the weeks following. Frank just sat there his mouth wide open, listening intently.

"Well, I'm happy for you," he said. "Though that religious stuff isn't for me, I'm glad to see you've found some peace and happiness. Lord knows we didn't really have any, did we?"

"No, and that was my fault," Martha replied. "I'm sorry, Frank. I'm the one that drove you away into another woman's arms, and I regret that."

Frank grabbed Martha's hand, "I was wrong too, no matter what you did. I'm sorry for betraying you. I didn't enjoy hurting you, I really didn't. I was just so mad and it was all about me, plain and simple."

For a minute Martha almost felt like hugging him, though that thought left her quickly.

"Well," Martha stood up, "I've got an appointment and you've got a baby and wife to see. Please give her my congratulations."

"Thanks," Frank said, grabbing Martha and hugging her before she realized. "I did love you, Martha, and I hope you know that."

"I know," Martha said. "I loved you too, but what's done is done. Now that we've forgiven one another, we can go on with our lives."

Frank smiled for the first time, "I wish the very best for you, Martha, and if there's anything I can do, please let me know. In fact," Frank stopped mid-sentence, "I've been feeling bad that I didn't give you what I owed you in our divorce proceedings. So, you can expect a check in the mail in a few days. That is, if you'll give me your address."

"Oh, you don't have to do that. You won fair and square in the courtroom," Martha replied.

"Let's just say, it would make me feel better," Frank grinned.

As they both parted, Martha sensed she was heading towards a new beginning and that God was confirming it step by step.

Victoria Lynn Deviney

Chapter 32

Henry's nurse pushed him out in a wheelchair, while Claire walked beside him. "It's so good to be out in the fresh air and sunshine again," Henry said, as he looked up and breathed in deeply.

"I bet so," Claire smiled, as she helped him into the waiting car.

"Where are we going to stay tonight?" Henry asked, as Claire eased out onto the freeway.

"Well, Marisa said we could stay at her home. She's on a business trip and won't be back for a couple of days."

"Oh," Henry said as he looked out the window.

"Is that OK?" Claire looked at him, "I guess I should have asked you first."

"Yes, I just don't want her to feel sorry for me. Finding out that David died has been hard enough. I don't need to have my only daughter thinking she has to take care of a sick old man."

"Well, I'm sure Marisa is feeling bad that she told you the news about David that way. But I don't think she feels that way," Claire looked over at him.

"Well, I appreciate Marisa letting us stay at her house, none the less," Henry smiled.

"What you need is some rest," Claire said. "Then perhaps we can continue our trip?"

"Maybe, but I'm not really sure, Claire. So far, it's been a disaster. One daughter who barely speaks to me and another son who is dead—then my heart attack. I'm beginning to think the Lord wants me to just pack up and go home."

"At least I tried to complete my challenge. You know that for a fact," Henry looked intently into Claire's eyes.

"I know, but I really feel that we need to stay here until Marisa comes home, and then go on to see your other son. "What's his name again?"

"Tom," Henry replied. "He lives in New York. I'm not sure I'm up to driving that far. Maybe we should just fly there instead. What do you think?"

"Sure, I think it would be easier on you," Claire nodded in agreement.

"Well, here we are," she said, as they pulled into the driveway.

Henry whistled as he looked out at the expansive lawn with the gated fence.

Claire rung the bell, and a man's voice came on asking for their names.

After they went through the massive gate into the circular driveway, the same man greeted them and took their suitcases into the house.

"Wow, what a home," Claire commented, as they walked into the foyer.

Henry just shook his head and looked around. Suddenly Marisa came out of the room adjacent to the living area. Shocked to see her, Henry reached out and hugged her. "I thought you were gone on a trip?" he said, as he wiped his eyes.

"Well, I told Claire to tell you that just in case I had to go; but luckily I got out of it this time."

"I'm so glad," Henry smiled.

"You have a beautiful home," Claire said, as she looked around at all the ornate paintings on the walls.

"Thank you," Marisa smiled. "It's comfortable, but I usually stay at my condo in the city during the week and make this my weekend get-away. Anyway, let's get you two into your bedrooms so you can rest Dad. And then we can have lunch outside in the garden later if you would like?"

"Oh, that sounds nice," Henry replied, "I am a little tired. Perhaps I'll go lay down a while if you don't mind?"

"Not at all, I've got some calls to make for work. Why don't we meet down here in an hour or so?"

"That would be great," Claire said, as she took Marisa's hand in hers. "You are very kind to let us stay with you for a few days."

"Well, it's the least I could do since I was the culprit of making dad have a heart attack," she frowned."

"Nonsense," Henry said, "It was coming on, don't think you caused it. However, I do wish you had told me about David when it happened. But that's in the past now.

"I'm sorry Dad. Tom and I should have told you. Anyway, I will see you two in a little while," and she walked back into the den.

Martha walked into the hospital room as Maggie and Trent were praying. Standing still, she bowed her head and thanked God for seeing Frank and being able to complete her challenge without even having to plan it. Looking up, she noticed that they were both smiling at her.

"Oh, so sorry," Martha said. "I came in when you two were praying, so I joined you."

"That's wonderful!" Maggie said, and reached out to take her hand. "We are both so glad you were able to come see us today. We have a favor to ask of you."

"Oh, what is it?" Martha said slowly.

"Both Trent and I are in need of someone to come and help me when I get back home. And as I prayed about it, your name kept coming to my mind."

"Yes," Trent continued. "I need to have a person there we can both trust to not only help Maggie, but little Jacob as well."

"Also, if you could do some light cleaning and cooking, that would be great too," Maggie smiled.

"Wow," Martha sat down to take it all in. "I've never done anything like that before. I have a couple of interviews lined up for tomorrow. But I've been praying and feeling that the Lord might have something different in mind for me … so perhaps this is from Him? Would you mind if I pray about it and get back to you?"

"We wouldn't have it any other way," Maggie spoke up. "In fact, I will be in the rehab hospital for a few weeks. That will give you time to see if this is something you would like to do."

"I'll get back to you before that," Martha smiled. "Also, thank you for thinking of me. I'm flattered that you would entrust me with this. The Lord is for sure moving quickly in my life these days," Martha laughed.

"Well, He tends to do that at times," Trent smiled.

"Yes," Maggie said. "Even in times of hardship as well."

Martha reached over to hug Maggie, "You sure have been through it. It's amazing to see how good you look, considering just last week we weren't even sure you were going to make it."

"I know, "Maggie said, and looked over at Trent. "I've felt the prayers of everyone, and they sure moved the heart of God."

"If you had asked me just a month ago what I would be doing; this wouldn't have even been on my radar screen," Martha said.

With that, Trent took Maggie's hand and asked her to pray with them thanking God for weaving all of their lives together.

◆ ◆ ◆

Henry, Claire, and Marisa were chatting out in the garden enjoying their sandwiches, when someone came up from behind and put his hand on Henry's shoulder. Startled he turned around to see his eldest son, Tom standing there. "Good heavens, you scared me to death!" Henry said and jumped up to give his son a bear hug.

"Whoa, not so hard, Dad, I can't get my breath!"

"How in the world did you know I was here?"

Tom looked over and winked at Marisa. "Your daughter put this together when you were in the hospital. She felt so bad after your heart attack she called me that night to see if I could possibly fly down."

"I don't know what to say," Henry sat down and looked over at Marisa. Wiping the tears from his eyes, he whispered, "Thank you," and she looked down at her plate.

"You're welcome, Dad. I have to apologize for my rudeness at the beginning. I'm still working through some unforgiveness."

"I understand," he patted her hand. "I was a fool, and it took a long time for the Lord to show me this, but it was too late to bring you all back to me. I've regretted it ever since. Now look, I have my two children right here with me."

Tom reached over and grabbed his dad's hand. "Look Dad, I've forgiven you, I really have. I should have contacted you sooner, but life got busy, and, well ... "

"I understand Son, I do. Come sit down and tell me about yourself."

No one noticed when Claire got up and walked back inside the house. Looking out at Henry and his children she smiled and realized that he had completed his challenge after all. Though there may be some bumpy roads ahead, she felt sure he, and the Lord, could handle them.

Unforeseen

Chapter 33

Martha's head was spinning as she walked out of the hospital. The prospect of doing something so different was scary yet exciting at the same time. She wasn't quite sure if she really wanted to do this, and she whispered to the Lord to please help her if this was what He had for her. Sensing this was just something temporary, she prayed for continued guidance.

A little voice inside her spoke to her heart and said, *trust me*. She stopped and looked around to see if anyone else heard it. Seeing everyone walking by unaware, she realized it was the Lord, who had spoken, and tears formed in her eyes.

So, is this how you communicate Lord? If so, then please help me to keep hearing your voice. I don't want to go my own way anymore.

Trent looked at his wife sleeping and opened up his Bible. Secretly hoping Martha would accept the job, he realized he only wanted the person the Lord had in mind. His eye dropped down to Proverbs 3:5-7, "Trust in the Lord with all your heart and lean not on your own understanding; in all your ways submit to Him, and He will make your paths straight."

Interesting, he thought as he laid his head back on the chair, *just what I needed to hear!* Suddenly the anxiety left him, and peace filled his heart. As he drifted off to sleep, a thought entered his mind to call the pastor, and to ask him about the deacons' meeting, and if they had made a decision about his six-month sabbatical. Wondering where that'd come from, he woke up with a start.

"What?" his wife raised up from her pillow.

"Oh Honey, I'm sorry, didn't mean to wake you. Was just reading my Bible, when I had a thought to call my pastor and ask about the decision from the deacons' meeting."

"Really," she sat up smiling. "Perhaps the Lord brought it to your mind then. Don't you think it's time?"

Seeing that familiar challenge in her eyes, he laughed and said, "Yeah, I guess so!"

"In fact, why don't you go on into work and ask him in person? I'm fine really. I'm going to be eating lunch soon, so come back this evening and tell me the good news!"

Reaching down to give her a big kiss, Trent smiled. "OK, I'm not going to argue with you this morning!"

"Good," Maggie said as she took his hand in hers, "because I don't want to waste my energy doing that anyway," and she pushed him away from the bed.

"OK, OK, I'm going," Trent grinned. "I will call you when I hear something."

Maggie smiled and shut her eyes again.

Walking down the familiar hall towards the elevator, Trent stopped and looked back towards Maggie's room, *Well I guess there's no harm in asking*, he thought. Silently, he thanked the Lord again for allowing Maggie to live.

Unforeseen

Terry heard her phone chirp and fumbled through her pocketbook. "Hello," she said."

"Hey Hon, it's your mom."

"Oh, hi," she said, a little exasperated.

"Are you OK, Honey? You sound a little stressed.

"Well, it isn't exactly the best day to talk mom. What's up?"

"Oh, I just wanted to let you know that the lake house is opened and ready for us to enjoy, whenever you can come up."

"Oh Mom, I don't know. I've called off the wedding, and Jeffery's giving me the two-week honeymoon he's already paid for. So, I think I going to take him up on it and go to the Caribbean next month." The phone was silent for a moment. "Mom, are you there?"

"Yes, Honey, I'm just surprised that's all. What happened? Why did you call off the wedding?"

"I can't get into it right now. I'm on my way to meet a client and to show houses for the rest of the day. Can we talk later this evening? I promise I'll call when I get home."

"Sure Honey. Sorry to have bothered you. I'll wait to hear from you."

"Thanks for calling Mom," Terry said and then she dropped the phone down into her purse, realizing that she was going to have to talk with her mom whether she liked it or not.

Trent walked into the church and noticed everyone was already gone. Looking down at his watch he realized it was 1:00pm, and that he was late. Sitting down, he took a look at his calendar and saw his week was full of meetings and youth activities. As he looked out his window into the parking lot, he saw Pastor Jeff coming up the sidewalk.

"Well, it's now or never," he said to himself. Feeling the stress come back, he again recited the verse the Lord had given him that morning. "Trust in The Lord with all my heart, help me not to lean on my own understanding, but in all my ways, acknowledge you, and you will direct my path." *Oh Lord, please direct my path,* he mumbled to himself.

"Hey there," Pastor Jeff said sticking his head in the door. "How is Maggie?"

"Oh, she's doing great. Thanks so much for your prayers! She will be going to rehab for a few weeks, but after that, we hope to get her home."

"That's great to hear. Great to hear."

"By the way," Trent said, as he got up and moved towards the door. "I wanted to ask what the deacon board decided about me taking a six-month leave."

"Oh that," Pastor Jeff said half-heartedly. "We never discussed it after Maggie's wreck. We figured you would be so busy taking care of her that you wouldn't need any additional time off. You have been out quite a lot," he said, as he patted his back.

Trent felt his stomach drop. "Oh, I see. I was planning on making that time up, especially since I've got several retreats scheduled that will require me to spend a few nights away."

"Well there's not another meeting until the first of next month. If you're still wanting the sabbatical, then I suggest you speak to Tim Elmore. He's the head deacon, and he will see if they can put it back on the agenda. But like I said, I wouldn't get my hopes up."

"I understand, just wanted to ask that's all," Trent smiled stiffly. "Well, better get back to work. Got a lot to do between now and Sunday."

"I understand," Pastor Jeff replied. "You have a good afternoon and please give Maggie a big hug for me and tell her that I will be up to see her on Friday!"

"Sure will," Trent said as he shut the door. *Well, that went well,* he thought to himself. *I'm not sure I even need to bring it up to Tim. Maybe I should just drop it, and let it ride for a while. At least until Maggie gets settled in, and things get back to normal. Then I will probably need a vacation.* Yet he still had a nagging feeling in the back of his mind, *that maybe I need to take a step of faith and just see what the Lord would do.*

Chapter 34

Terry walked in the door kicking off her shoes. "Hello," she said, but no one answered. *Good, she thought to herself, I need a moment of solitude*, as she sat down on her comfy sofa. She laid back against the pillow and closed her eyes thinking about how much things had changed since she'd received that weird phone call about an inheritance.

As she thought about the wedding and not getting married, she felt a sadness. But she also realized she hadn't missed Jeffery at all. "Well at least I had the sense to know when to call it quits instead of having to go through a divorce like most of my friends," she said out loud.

But something deeper was bothering her. Something about what her counselor had said about this Jesus, and also seeing how Martha was changing too. I wonder, she sat thinking, *perhaps there is something to this Jesus*. Just then she remembered she'd told her mom that she would call her. Pulling her phone out of her purse, she quickly dialed the familiar number.

"Hello," her mom answered on the first ring.

Unforeseen

"Hi, Mom. I finally got home and wanted to give you a call before my roommate comes in."

"Oh, I'm so glad you did Honey! How did your showings go today?"

"The usual, people have big expectations, and I've got to get them down to reality, so it takes a while."

"I understand. Listen I was thinking I could come down next week, and we could have dinner one evening. I'll stay at the new hotel, so no need to stress about the lodging. What do you think dear?"

"That would be fine, mom. But I don't want you to be driving so far alone."

"I'll be fine Honey. I've got my phone, and I will call if I have any trouble."

"Alright then, why don't we make it Friday evening, I usually get off a little earlier, and we can meet say around 5:30?"

"Sounds great, I appreciate it Honey. Will call you when I get checked in at the hotel, if that's OK?"

"Sure, so you're staying at the new Omni hotel downtown?"

"Yes, I believe it's in the city center."

"It is, and really nice too. They've got a lovely restaurant where we can eat. I will meet you in the lobby at 5:30 then."

"Great, see you soon, Dear, and get some rest this weekend!"

"Sure, Mom, you too."

As Terry laid her head back again on the pillow, she realized everything was working out right on time.

Trent dialed Tim's number. Nervous, he heard the cell click into background music. "Hello," a voice answered.

"Mr. Elmore, this is Trent Drew from the church."

"Oh yes, Trent, how can I help you?"

"Sorry to bother you, but I wanted to ask you if you might be able to add my request for a sabbatical to your deacons' meeting agenda again, maybe for next month? I just spoke to Pastor Jeff, and he told me to call you since you are the head deacon."

"I see," Tim said quietly. "I know your wife's been very ill. Has she taken a turn for the worse?"

"No, in fact, she's doing very well, and she will be transferred to a rehab hospital in a few days."

"That's great. So, is the leave of absence to help her when she returns home?"

"Actually no. I've been feeling like the Lord is leading me to take a six-month leave to spend some time with Him and get recharged. This was in place before my wife even had the wreck."

"I see," Tim said quietly. "Well, Trent, all I can do as chairman is to bring this up and see what the other men think. Send it to me either by email, or let's try to see each other on Sunday morning."

"Thanks, I will, Mr. Elmore, and I really appreciate it."

"I have one question before we hang up, Trent."

"Sure," Trent said.

"Are you happy with your position at the church, or has something happened to make you feel like you need a break?"

"Actually, it all came about several weeks ago when I received word about an inheritance I and a few others were given. We each had a challenge to complete, and mine was to ask for a six-month leave."

Unforeseen

"Interesting," Tim replied. "So, are you hoping to get enough money not to have to work?"

"No, not at all. In fact, there are three more people that are also getting a part of this inheritance, whatever sum it may end up being. Personally, I don't think it's a lot, but what I've learned from meeting with this group is to trust the Lord more, and to take more risks, in an effort to grow closer to Him."

"I see, Tim paused, "well, like I said, just put this request in writing and give it to me on Sunday, and we'll see what we can do."

"Thank you, Sir, I really appreciate it" Trent said. After he hung up he noticed that he hadn't been breathing, and so he took a deep breath. *Lord I did it,* he thought, *I may lose my job, but at least I took a step of faith!*

Martha walked in the door to find Terry asleep on the couch. She went into the kitchen to fix some dinner when she heard Terry stirring. "Hello?" Terry said.

"Sorry," Martha said, as she walked into the living room. "You were out when I came in. Didn't mean to disturb you."

"No, you didn't. Can't believe I fell asleep! Guess I was tired," she said laughing. "What are you fixing?"

"I'm not sure. I was just looking to see what I could throw together."

"Why don't we order out?" Terry said.

"OK, what are you in the mood for?" Martha grinned.

"How about sushi?"

"Really? They bring sushi to your door?"

"Yup, we could order some Chinese food too."

Martha tried the sushi first and said, "Not bad, but I still think I'll have the Chinese," and she grabbed more of the sweet and sour chicken.

Laughing, Terry asked about Martha's time with Trent and Maggie.

"Oh, you'll never believe what they asked me! They want me to help out with Maggie after she is able to come home."

"What?" Terry stopped eating and looked at Martha. "Are you experienced in that sort of work?"

"Not really, but it's just helping her get around, and taking care of the house, and watching Jacob too."

"Wow, that's a lot, Martha. You sure you want to do that?"

"It's not really something I've ever done, but I sense the Lord wants me to do something a little uncomfortable … and different for a change."

"I see," Terry said as she put another bite of the raw fish in her mouth.

"Is something wrong?" Martha asked.

"Oh, nothing. I was just thinking about our little group—how we all are doing and experiencing things we wouldn't have ever thought before."

"True," Martha smiled, "especially me! I mean, look how I used to be not so very long ago," she said thoughtfully. "But I wouldn't change this for anything in the world. I used to think happiness consisted of things, but now there's only one thing important to me."

"What's that?" Terry looked into her eyes.

"Well, I don't want to sound too religious, but for me it's doing what the Lord wants me to do and getting myself out of the way—not being so self-centered."

"I see," Terry said thoughtfully. "I guess I'm just not ready to make that kind of commitment, not yet anyway."

"And you shouldn't until you are," Martha smiled warmly. "Love is a choice, and God gives us a free will to accept his invitation for a love relationship. We can't demand anyone love us, and God doesn't want that either."

"Well, that's good to hear," Terry said, as she stood up. "I'm stuffed, I think I will go and clean up the kitchen."

"Let me help," Martha said, as she picked up the empty plates. "Maybe will have time to watch a movie!"

"Sounds good to me," Terry said, as she cleared the table, secretly envying her friend's peace.

Chapter 35

Henry sat there taking everything in as his children talked. "So, Dad tell us why you are here?" Tom turned to look his dad in the eyes.

"Well Son, it's an interesting story if both of you have time to listen."

Tom looked over to Marisa and smiled. "Sure dad, we have time," Marisa spoke first.

"Well, Marisa knows part of the story. I had an interesting phone call not long ago telling me that I had inherited some money … from a Mr. Peterson," Tom finished up his sentence.

Both Henry and Marisa looked at Tom. "How did you know what I was going to say?" Henry asked as he sat forward in his chair.

"Yes, how in the world would you know about this?" Marisa said, "unless you both have something going on I don't know about?"

Tom shook his head, "No, Marisa. Listen both of you. I'm sorry I interrupted, but I know about this Mr. Peterson because my wife had the same phone call about a year ago."

"Really?" they both said at the same time.

Unforeseen

"But Katy is dead now," Marisa said, "did this have something to do with it?"

"Yes, and No," Tom stood up and looked out over the lake.

Henry just sat, then he said quietly, "Tom, when did your wife die? I hadn't heard. I'm so sorry."

"About a year now, but the children and I are doing OK. We still miss her badly, but I know where she is, so that gives me comfort."

"Are you a Christian?" Henry smiled broadly.

"Yes, Dad, I am. If it weren't for my faith, I would have never gotten through this year."

Marisa squirmed uncomfortably. "Listen you two, if this is going to be some kind of hallelujah session, I'm out of here."

Both Tom and Henry stopped mid-sentence, and just looked at Marisa. "Don't look at me like that," she said, "I'm not the one who's the religious nut. I'm spiritual, just not in the way you both seem to be."

"We understand Honey," Henry smiled. "Sorry to have made you uncomfortable."

"Anyway, Tom, please continue on with your story," Henry nodded.

Tom talked about the details of Katy's particular challenge, her ministry at the women's shelter, and the day her life was taken by one of the abusive husbands. Henry just sat there speechless.

"I wish I had known, Tom," Henry spoke. "Maybe I could have helped in some way."

"I know. I wish you could have been with me too. But I was too devastated to think during that time. But the Lord knew what was going to take place way before we did, and Katy died knowing that she had fulfilled her lifelong desire and God's will for her life. Besides the work is still going on and growing by leaps and bounds!" Tom smiled.

"So, who has taken over the shelters then?" Marisa spoke up

"One of the other ladies that was in the group. I believe there was four of them."

"Yes," Henry said, "apparently that's the number, because we have four as well."

"So," Marisa said slowly, "this inheritance thing is more than just about the money?"

"Yes," Tom and Henry said at the same time.

"When Katy first told me about it, at the beginning, I thought it was a scam. But we both quickly realized there was something deeper going on. Then she came home and revealed her lifelong dream of helping abused women. Well, that's when I told her not to accept this challenge. I was afraid of what might happen."

"And rightly so," Henry chimed in.

"But I also realized that if I didn't let her at least try and make this dream happen, she would have always held that against me."

"I seem to remember you telling me something about it last year, but I had no idea it was because of this," Marisa said quietly.

"Well, I wanted Katy to be happy and fulfilled. I had to step back and let her try, and she was wonderful. You should have seen the way she organized the shelters and prayed about those who she needed to help her and to be on her board. I never knew she had all those abilities and organizational skills." Tom's voice trailed off as if remembering that time.

"Son, "Henry said as he put his hand on his leg," "I've missed so much of your lives. I know we can't get back the past, and I wouldn't want to, at least not the way I was before. But I sure would like to be in both of your lives from now on, That is, if you would be open to it?"

Both Tom and Marisa just sat there. Tom was the first to get up and hug his dad. "Yes, Dad, I need you in my life, I don't know why I didn't try to find you after all this happened. But I didn't know you had changed, or even if you were alive. I've always loved you, I never stopped. I would love for you to be a part of our lives!" Both men just laughed and cried at the same time and didn't even notice Marisa slipping away and going inside the house.

Trent was surprised to see Terry coming up the sidewalk. "Hey there!" he called out, and she threw up her hand. "Are you coming to see Ron?"

"Yes, but I don't have an appointment. Just thought I would check to see if he was available."

"There's no one here, I'm sorry to say. I'm the last one leaving tonight."

"Oh, I see. Well, that's OK. It was just a spur of the moment thought."

"I would be glad to stay and talk to you, but I'm on my way to see Maggie. Then I have to get home to Jacob."

"No, that's OK!" Terry said and started to walk away. Trent sensed something was bothering her.

"Listen, how about following me to the hospital and having some dinner with Maggie and me? She would love some girl company!"

Terry stopped and thought a minute. "Sure, why not! I would love to see her too, it's been a while, and Martha said she was doing great."

"She is. Then if you would like, we can talk there?"

"OK," Terry smiled. "I'll meet you there. Let me stop and get us some take-out, I'm sure you both would like some different food. Wouldn't you? I know hospital food gets old fast."

"Sounds like a plan," Trent said. "I sure would like a pizza, what about you?"

"Sounds great, and I know just the place."

As they both walked their separate ways, Trent eagerly hoped Terry was ready to talk more about spiritual things.

Chapter 36

Martha came home to find the house dark, and no one home. Thinking this might just be a good time to think and pray about Trent and Maggie's job offer, she threw her purse down on the table and looked into the fridge, only to see some cheese and turkey. *Looks like a grilled cheese and turkey night to me*, she laughed to herself. She put the butter into the pan and began to pour herself a glass of juice, when suddenly a thought hit her, and she stopped what she was doing.

Looking out the bay window over the deck, the full moon that had been hiding behind the trees majestically appeared and the glow made a silhouette of a cross.

"That's so beautiful," she whispered and felt a stirring down deep in her heart. At first she wasn't sure what it meant, but then she knew it was the Lord speaking to her. The peace that enveloped her was like the old robe her mom used to put on her as a child—all warm, soft and secure.

Later she cut her sandwich in half and sat down at the table. Bowing her head, she thanked the Lord for her food, and the answer of a job that allowed her to live out her newfound faith in a more practical way.

Terry walked into the hospital foyer with the pizza and a little extra surprise for dessert. Not finding the elevator, she asked the first person who came her way. Realizing that he was a doctor, she felt her cheeks flush and the redness climbing up her neck.

"Oh, follow me," he smiled and led her down the long hall. "So many people get lost here, don't worry," he turned around and grinned again.

The first thing she noticed was his dimples, and then his eyes that twinkled. "Thank you," she stumbled over her words. "I've only been here once, and to tell you the truth I'm directionally challenged, to say the least."

He laughed loudly, and Terry looked around to see if anyone was listening. "Sorry," he commented. "I tend to laugh too loud, that's one thing my peers tell me to watch while I'm doing my rounds. But what they think doesn't worry me too much! Besides, in a place like this, everyone needs a little joy, or else it would be too depressing, don't you think?"

"Why, I guess so—come to think of it," and she laughed too.

"Where are you heading?" he asked, as he stepped onto the elevator with her. "I can help you carry something. It looks like you're feeding an army," he grinned.

Smiling she again blushed. "Just visiting some friends, who were in the mood for something other than the hospital buffet."

"I can understand that," he nodded. "That's a very thoughtful thing to do and he looked at her a little too intently.

Unforeseen

Fidgeting, Terry began to look up at the door to see how many more floors she needed to go. "What floor?" he said noting her nervousness.

"It's the eighth floor," she replied.

"Hey, that's where I'm heading too." And as they both stepped off they realized they were walking in the same direction. "Who did you say you were visiting?" he looked over at her.

"I didn't," she said and grinned, but if you must know it's Maggie and Trent Bowers."

"Really?" The doctor stopped mid-sentence. "That's just who I'm going to see as well!"

"In that case then, you may carry some of my load," and they both smiled as they walked into the room.

Trent stood up when he saw Dr. Nelson, but he was surprised to see Terry coming in right after him carrying food. Maggie sat there grinning in her bed looking back and forth at the both of them.

"Well," Trent said, "not only do doctors make evening visits, they also bring food with them!"

Laughing Dr. Nelson and Terry just shrugged and recounted their meeting downstairs. "So maybe if I'm good," Dr. Nelson added, "then I can stay for a few minutes longer and eat some pizza too!"

"Absolutely," Trent grinned, "we would be honored."

Maggie patted the foot of her bed and motioned for Terry to come and sit. Trent meanwhile took the food over to the small table near the window. Dr. Nelson began to examine Maggie, and Terry walked over towards the door to speak to Trent. As they talked, Trent's phone started to buzz in his pocket. "Excuse me," he said and walked out of the room. "Hello?"

"Trent, it's Martha. "Am I disturbing you?"

"No, not at all, in fact Terry just got here. She brought us some dinner, and Dr. Nelson is examining Maggie."

"Is everything all right?" Martha asked.

"Oh, yes, I believe this will be the last time. Hopefully they'll be discharging her to go to rehab tomorrow."

"That's sounds wonderful. But if I may ask, why is Terry there?"

"Oh, we met at the church, and I invited her to come and have some dinner with us. I'm hoping we can also talk some more."

"Oh, that's great," Martha exclaimed! "I will be praying. Well, the reason why I called is that I believe I just got confirmation from the Lord a little while ago. I think I am supposed to take the job with you all."

"Really! That's awesome," Trent said. "Can't wait to tell Maggie!"

"I think I will come up tomorrow, and if Maggie's still around, discuss my job description with both of you."

"Sure," Trent said. "In fact, I will talk to her tonight and see if we can get some things down on paper to give you."

"Great. Well, I will let you get back to your dinner, and I can't wait to hear the good news!"

"Appreciate you praying," Trent replied.

"Praying now," Martha said. As she clicked off her phone she silently asked the Lord for Terry's healing and salvation.

Chapter 37

As Trent came back into the room he saw that the pizza was half eaten. "Well, I step out a minute and the food disappears," he said grinning.

Maggie smiled and looked over at Terry. "What can I say Honey, I've gotten my appetite back!"

Terry handed him a big piece, and he sat down to eat while they continued their conversation. *It sure was good to see things almost back to normal,* though he knew they still had a long way to go. As he thought about his challenge, he prayed a quick prayer that the deacons would be led by the Lord, and not their pocketbooks.

Getting up, he excused himself and took another piece of pizza. He felt led to walk down the hall. Glancing into some of the rooms, he noticed many were dark and silent, while others were full of family members. It seemed the Lord was trying to show him something, but he just couldn't put his finger on it.

Lord, what is it you're trying to say to me? I'm not understanding it, he said to himself.

Then he began to notice how each person in those rooms represented a life, one that was important to God. It was at that moment, Trent heard the question—first silently, then loud and clear what the next step in his life would be. His heart pounding in his ears, he didn't even hear Terry come up behind him and ask if he had time to talk. As she tapped on his shoulder he literally jumped, and she stepped back quickly.

"Are you all right?" Terry said quietly.

"Sorry," Trent said, "I was just deep in thought and didn't hear you come up."

"That's OK, I think I talked Maggie's ear off, so I wondered if you had a minute before I go?"

"All the time in the world," he smiled. "Why don't we go over near the elevator?" As they sat down, Trent noticed Terry wringing her hands. "Are you OK?" he asked.

"I just have a lot on my mind," Terry replied. "I'm supposed to go see my mom this weekend, and I still haven't talked to her about the botched abortion."

"I kinda understand how you feel," Trent shook his head. "I haven't completed my challenge either. Are you afraid of bringing this up to your mom?"

"Well, I wasn't at first. But when I saw her at my wedding shower, she was like a different person, and it unnerved me. I'm not sure what's going on with her—she's a lot nicer, and normal acting."

"Well, that can't be a bad thing then can it?" Trent chuckled.

"Guess not. But now that's she's "normal", I kinda like her, and I don't want to mess it up."

"I see your point," Trent looked out the window. Looking back at Terry, he took a deep breath. "Listen, Terry, I know you've spoken to Ron about all of this, since he's your counselor. What has he advised you to do?"

"To pray and not rush into doing or saying anything I shouldn't."

Unforeseen

"And you haven't, have you?" Trent kept looking into her eyes.

"No, I haven't. But I'm sensing that now I just need to do it and let the chips fall where they may."

"Then I think you've got your answer. Let's pray for the right moment, and for God to prepare your mom's heart for the discussion."

As Terry bowed her head, she sensed another presence near them as Trent called upon his Lord yet again. When Trent looked up, he noticed Terry was crying. "What is it Terry?" Trent grabbed his handkerchief out if his back pocket and gave it to her.

"It's that familiar presence again when you prayed. I can't put my finger on it, but it's comforting—something I've never felt before."

"What you've been feeling is the Lord. He's the one who created you, loves you, and has a plan for your life, Terry. But until you come to know Him personally, He can't reveal that to you. Are you ready now to ask Him into your heart?"

Terry looked down a minute and said nothing. Then she heard it ... a voice, not audible, but so loud it made her ears tingle. She instantly knew there was a God out there who loved her. He had just said that to her. It was as if her eyes were opened for the first time, and she knew deep down that God had saved her from the abortion that should have killed her.

As she looked up Trent was smiling. "Did you hear that?" Terry whispered.

"Hear what?" Trent said.

"You didn't hear that voice?"

"No, what did it say?"

"I heard someone say that He had always loved me."

"He does," Trent grinned, "and He wants to be the father you never had, if you'll let him. Now, are you ready?

"Yes," she said and bowed her head.

Henry laid down late that night and silently thanked the Lord for allowing him to be able to see his children again after all these years. He prayed for both Tom and Marisa, then drifted off to sleep dreaming of his family and the happy times to come.

Marisa was pouring herself a drink when Tom came into the room. "You're up late," he grinned. "What happened to you at dinner? We looked up, and you were gone."

"Well, it seemed that you and Dad were in another world. So, I went in to finish up some work I had to do in the office. I'm done now and decided to calm myself down before bed."

Tom sat down in the big leather chair. "So, what's up with you these days sis? I haven't kept in touch very well since Katy's death, and I'm sorry for that."

"Nothing much. Just travel, work, and more work," she sighed and took another sip of her drink.

"I was thinking," Tom said as he leaned forward, "why don't you come and visit the girls and me over the holidays this year? I have plenty of room, and now that my work is local, I'm there more."

"I don't know. Frank wants me to travel with him overseas this year, and frankly I think I need a change of scenery."

"Well, Frank is invited too, if you want him to come with you. But it's been a long time since we've all been together, and I miss that. Maybe we could even invite Dad too?"

With that Marisa got up and poured herself another glass of wine. "Listen Tom, you and Dad can get all chummy, and talk about your "faith", but that's not me and it never will be. I live in the present and don't think about the past. I've lived without a father for most of my life, and I have no desire to have one now."

Tom just sat there quietly praying. "Marisa, you have always had a mind of your own. You're a smart girl, and very successful. I'm not trying to persuade you to forgive Dad, and for us to be one big happy family all of a sudden. But why not give him the benefit of the doubt, and at least open up your heart to being cordial. He's an old man and won't live forever."

Marisa just sat there thinking about all the holidays, and birthdays when she had longed to see her dad, and tears welled up in her eyes. "I don't know. I just can't make that decision right now, but I'll think about it OK?"

"That's my girl," Tom gave Marisa a big hug.

"Stop," she said laughing and pushed him away. "What's got into you! You haven't done that in a long time."

"Sorry, it's just a habit," he said and planted a big kiss on her cheek.

Rolling her eyes, she smiled, and said, "So, you wore me down a little, but don't think I'm going to become a 'holy roller' like you two!"

Grinning, Tom said, "Don't worry, I'm not in the business of saving anyone. The Lord will do that Himself."

With that Marisa reached back to turn the lights off, and they headed off to bed.

Chapter 38

Terry hugged both Trent and Maggie and picked up her pocketbook. "Guess I better leave," she said, "didn't mean to stay so long!"

"Nonsense," Maggie said. "We are both so excited for you, and we will be praying for you and your mom this weekend!"

"Thanks," Terry smiled, "will let you know how it all goes."

As Maggie drifted off to sleep, Trent sat staring out the window for a long time, thanking God for Terry's newfound faith and praying for clarity and direction in his life as well. Sensing a new calling and ministry, he wondered how Maggie would handle it. He sure didn't want to add any more stress on her. If this was indeed something the Lord was doing, then the long-awaited six-month sabbatical wouldn't be necessary after all.

Trent got up from his chair, kissed Maggie on the cheek, picked up his coat and headed out the door. "Where do you think you're going?" Maggie opened one eye.

"I thought you were asleep! You need to rest, we've worn you out tonight!"

"I'm great, just needed to take a quick nap," she said quietly, pushing herself up on the pillow "You've got something else on your mind, don't you?"

"Why would you say that?"

"Honey, I've known you for almost ten years now, I think I can tell when something is bothering you. Is it our finances? Are we OK for me to go to rehab? If not, I'm sure we can do something else."

"No, stop it. We're fine. The insurance is great, and we have so much to be thankful for, especially now that Martha's going to help once you get home!"

"Really? That's great. When did you find out?"

"She called tonight while you and Terry were talking."

"Then, what is it?" Maggie kept prodding as she usually did.

"Well, a weird thing happened tonight. When you and Terry were talking, I decided to just walk out in the hall to clear my mind."

"Go on," she sat up, listening intently.

"Well, I started to walk down the hall, glancing into some of the rooms. Then I began to pray for the patients and their families. I just had a sense that God was birthing something new in my life. Now, don't get me wrong, I do enjoy working at the church and with the kids. But tonight, well, it was as if God was pricking my spirit and giving me a new desire to help counsel families through a crisis, much like ours. Do you understand what I'm saying, Honey?"

Smiling, Maggie reached out to grab his hand, and pulled him towards her. "Yes, Honey, I believe I do. I've been watching you even before the accident happened and felt that God was preparing you for something else. I just didn't know what that might be. Who knew it would involve me and all of this," she said as she looked around the room. "But the Lord's ways aren't ours, and He does work out all things for our good, if we let Him."

"Well, maybe I will pray and fast about this, to get confirmation."

"Yes, that might be a good thing. But let's both start praying now and see how the Lord will work it all out."

"Thanks. Honey," Trent reached down and kissed her lightly on the lips. "I'm leaving now, so please get some rest! I'll be back sometime tomorrow."

"I think they're going to be moving me tomorrow afternoon, so why don't you call first and see where I am," Maggie smiled.

"Sure, thank you, My Love. Now please rest."

Trent walked out into the night air. He felt a strange calmness in spite of everything. Silently he prayed, *Lord, you alone know my steps, so please take me by the hand and lead me where you want me to be.*

Martha heard the key turn in the door and sat up. "Hi there," she said, as Terry came in.

"Hey, did I wake you?"

"I just dozed off while watching the news," Martha yawned. She eyed Terry and thought something looked different about her. "So, is everything ok?" Martha asked.

"Well, you won't believe what happened tonight!"

"What?" Martha asked.

"I went to see if I could meet with Ron this afternoon, and I ran into Trent who was going up to see Maggie and have supper with her. We got to talking and he invited me to come with him."

"So, Ron wasn't in?" Martha asked.

Unforeseen

"No, everyone was gone except for Trent. Seems they only work half a day on Fridays. Anyway, I decided I would pick up pizza for us, and we really had a nice time together. But in the midst of it all, Trent and I had a moment to talk, and the next thing I knew we were sitting down and talking about the Lord. Would you believe I asked God into my heart?"

"You did?" Martha said, and then got up to give her a big hug! "That's wonderful, I'm so excited! I knew you looked different when you came in! This calls for a celebration," Martha said, "and I know just what we need!"

"What?" Terry asked, following her into the kitchen.

"My homemade apple pie with ice cream!"

"I usually don't eat dessert," Terry shook her head.

"Well, can't you just this once?" Martha eyed her.

"I guess tonight I can make an exception!"

"Good, because I just made it. I was wanting something sweet," she laughed. "So, now are you ready to confront your mom?" Martha asked.

"I think so," Terry said taking a big bite of apple pie. "Wow, this is good, I might should eat sweets more often! Anyway, I think I have the strength to talk to her in an honest and loving way now. It's weird, as soon as I prayed tonight to Jesus, I immediately felt a peace about the whole situation."

"That's great," Martha smiled.

"So," Terry asked, "when do you start working for Maggie!"

"Well, she goes into the rehab hospital tomorrow for a couple of weeks, so after that I guess. That is unless Trent wants me to come over and take care of Jacob now."

"I see. Isn't it interesting how different our lives have turned out to be since we all met?" Terry commented.

"Yes, and we have two more weeks left," Martha said, as she got up to get herself another piece of pie. "Want some more?" she looked back at Terry.

"Sure, why not, I've already blown my diet anyway with that pizza I ate. But who cares, I'm not trying to get into a wedding dress now!"

Laughing, they both sat down and continued talking until they realized it was well past midnight.

Chapter 39

Claire woke early and wandered over to the window. "Just beautiful," she whispered, as she looked out at the well-manicured lawn with all its trees and flowers. It looks like something right out of a magazine. Then glancing over at the clock on the mantle, she saw that it was only 6:00am.

Would love a good cup of coffee right about now, she thought as she put on her sweat suit. Tiptoeing down the long hall, she came to the spiral staircase and heard someone stirring about downstairs. "Hello?" she said peeping into the kitchen as she saw Marisa's head in the refrigerator.

"Oh, hello there," Marisa said, looking up quickly. "You startled me, I'm usually the only one up this early!"

"Sorry, I woke up starving and thought I would come down to see if anyone else was."

"Well, I'm not much of a breakfast eater, but I did order some scones and bagels."

"That sounds heavenly," Claire smiled. "Can I help you with anything?"

"Oh, no thanks. I'm just going to fix some coffee, that is if you drink it. Otherwise I can do tea?"

"I absolutely love coffee in the morning," Claire smiled.

"Good, hope you like French press. That's all I do—coffee pots aren't my thing."

"Oh, that's fine. However you make it, I'm sure I will love it!"

Marisa looked at Claire for a moment, then turned around to pour the hot water into the carafe. "So, how long have you been seeing my dad?"

"Excuse me?" Claire replied.

"I mean, how long have you and Dad known each other? It seems you are an item." Marisa said smiling.

"Well, I got to know your Dad at the inheritance meetings, but I've known about your dad a long time. My deceased husband used to work for him many years ago."

"I see," Marisa grabbed the milk from the fridge.

"Yes, my husband used to come home talking about his work and his boss, and I knew his name, but had never met him. I was so surprised to see how very different he really was in person. I pictured an unapproachable man, who was totally businesslike."

"Well, you weren't far off base," Marisa said, handing her a cup of coffee. "The cream is here, and the sugar is on the table if you want some."

"Just cream, thanks," Claire said as she took the steaming cup.

"Anyway, dad was a busy man always working—no time for us. When he was around, his mind was always somewhere else. I used to think he was running around on my mom, and that perhaps he had a mistress or something. But I realized that his mistress was really his work."

As Marisa opened the box, she handed the scones to Claire. "I've got both butter and clotted cream for the toppings.

"Both sound delicious," Claire said, as she sat down at the table overlooking the terrace. "You certainly have a beautiful home, Marisa. I was looking out my window earlier and thought your yard and grounds look like something out of a magazine!"

Marisa turned to glance out the window, "Yes, it is pretty. No thanks to me. My gardener does a superb job for sure! Actually, my house was featured in a local magazine not long ago."

"So, I wasn't too far off then," Claire grinned taking a big bite of her scone.

"I don't get out here too often. I wish I did, but life and work are so busy. I usually stay in the city much more than I would like."

"You sound a lot like your dad," Claire said looking into Marisa's eyes.

"Yes, I'm afraid the apple doesn't fall too far from the tree," she smiled sadly.

"Well, you can change that, your dad did."

"Yes, but it's a little too late if you know what I mean," Marisa got up to pour herself another cup of coffee. "Would you like some more?"

"Sure, why not," Claire gave Marisa her empty cup. "But I have to disagree with your statement, Marisa. I don't think it's ever too late, as long as you're alive, things can change."

Marisa looked out over the pool, "Perhaps," she mumbled. "But I'm not sure I can. That's just not in my nature."

"I understand," Claire replied. "Forgiving another person isn't easy, because it goes against our flesh. But when you realize that forgiveness is really for you, not the other person, it makes it a little easier."

"Yes, that's what I've heard," Marisa said, as she sipped her coffee. "I don't dwell on the past, it takes too much energy. I try to just focus on the future instead."

"I see," Claire looked deep into her Marisa's eyes. "I think sometimes we choose not to deal with the past, but I don't think we ever forget it. Forgiveness says, 'All right, it happened. So, I can either stay stuck or move on toward the future.' Are you stuck Marisa?"

Marisa was silent, then looked up at Claire. "Do I look stuck to you?"

Claire noted a smugness in her voice. Looking down at her plate, Claire prayed and asked the Lord for the right words. "No, on the surface it looks like you've got it all together. You have a great job, beautiful homes, and lots of material things—and even a nice fiancé, from what I've seen. But you can still be stuck emotionally."

"Well, I hope you're not going to get all religious on me like Dad and Tom did last night. I told them, and I'll tell you that I'm not turning into some religious fanatic, nor do I need a counselor right now."

Sensing a wall, Claire took the conversation another way. "I'm not here to push God or therapy down your throat. Perhaps you need some healing in the area of your emotions, that's all. God can heal you. I know because He's healed me from losing my husband to cancer a few years ago, and He's gotten me through some other hard times in my life. But the choice to let Him in, is totally up to you. God gave us all free will. He loves us, but He's a gentleman and won't intrude into our lives, unless we open the door to let Him come in."

"Well, I'm just not ready nor am I interested at this time," Marisa said, as she got up and took her plate to the sink. Oh, I've got someone who comes to clean, so feel free to leave your dishes on the table. She usually gets here around 9:00am or so. It was nice talking to you Claire," Marisa tried to smile, "but I've got a phone call to make in my office, and another long day, so I better get to it."

"Well, thank you, Marisa, for the wonderful breakfast and coffee. I think I just might have to go out and buy me a French press!" she laughed.

"They are addictive. Once you've had coffee this way, nothing ever tastes the same," she smiled.

"Well, that's how it is with the Lord as well," Claire added. "Once you've tasted His love for you, there's nothing else quite like it."

Marisa turned around and looked her in the eyes, "I'm sure that is true for you."

Claire watched Marisa walk down the long hall towards the sunroom and into her office. Sighing, she prayed and asked the Lord to please allow someone else to come along and water those seeds that were being planted.

Chapter 40

Shutting the door of her office, Terry glanced over to the wall clock which let her know she was running late as usual. Calling her mom on the way to the car, she tapped her radio buttons until she found a Christian station. *Um, that's different; never heard this music before.* She found herself singing as she hit the freeway towards downtown.

Walking into the lobby, she looked around to see her mom already standing at the bar. Terry waved when her mom looked her way. Smiling, her mom raised her glass of wine. "Hey, Honey" her Mom hugged her tightly.

"Sorry I'm late as usual." Terry shrugged. "I had so many closings today." Her Mom smiled, "Oh, it's OK, really. I've enjoyed all the amenities here. I feel like I've been pampered all day!"

As they waited to be seated, Terry ordered a glass of tea. Honey, I already ordered you a red wine."

"Oh well, I just feel like a sweet tea tonight."

The waiter sat them at a round table over-looking the city. "Isn't this city beautiful at night," her mom said!

"Yes, I love living in it." Terry glanced out the window. As they looked over the menu, Terry's mouth began to water. "I heard their chicken and ribs are delicious," Terry said.

"Yes, I'm sure everything they have is good," her mom said, looking around. "It sure is busy tonight. Are the weekends always like this?"

Terry looked up and nodded, "It seems to be as popular as I've heard."

"So, Mom, how have you been doing lately?"

"Oh, I'm doing fine, Honey. How are you doing since the breakup?"

"I'm great; Jeffery and I are still friends, so that's been a blessing."

"Are you still going to the Caribbean next month?" her Mom asked.

"Yes, I'm so excited. I haven't been on a vacation like that in a long time."

"That's good, Honey. I'm happy that you're happy. My, these rolls are delicious!" her mom said, as she reached for another one.

"Yes, they are good, but I've got to stop eating them or else I won't be able to eat my chicken and ribs! So, Mom, how is your boyfriend?"

"Oh yes, I spoke to him a few minutes ago, he's doing great. He just may come up and spend the rest of the weekend with me. But that will still give us time by ourselves tonight, and if you have time in the morning, maybe we can do some shopping? "

"Maybe," Terry said slowly, "that is if I can get out of some showings. I'm glad I came down this evening though, she coughed. "I've been wanting to talk to you about something that's been on my mind."

"Oh really," her mom looked up. "Is there anything wrong?"

"Well, a lot has happened this summer. Guess I need to update you on everything."

"Please do," her Mom said, as she laid her napkin down. "I would love to hear all about your life. I've sensed you've had a lot going on lately."

Terry continued. "Well, first off, I received a call about an inheritance several weeks ago, and it required going to a few weekly meetings."

"Really?" her mom said, excited! "Who was it that gave you money?"

"Oh, a Mr. Peterson, you wouldn't know him. I barely met him one time."

"That sounds a little fishy, doesn't it?"

"Well, at first I thought it was a scam. But then as I began to get to know the others—"

"What others?" her Mom interrupted. "Are there more than one of you getting money?"

Just then the waiter came with the food. "Wow, this is a lot of food," Terry grinned and looked at her Mom.

Her Mom glanced over at Terry. "Sure is. We may need to take home some leftovers," her mom said, as she continued. "You said there are three others getting a part of this inheritance?"

"Yes", Terry replied as she took a big bite of the ribs. "Um delicious," she said wiping her mouth.

"So, what do you think is the reason for this inheritance?" her Mom asked.

"It's more than just an inheritance," Terry replied, a little frustrated.

"Well it's none of my business."

"Go ahead Mom, and tell me what you're thinking," Terry said again.

"I'm just wondering why there are four of you, that's all."

"I wondered that too, but it seems we all four met this man and somehow helped him, so he chose all of us, I guess. As I've gotten to know the other three, I realized that we all needed each other to get through our challenges together."

"Challenges?" Her mom looked at her questionably.

"Yes, that's one of the stipulations to receive the inheritance. We each had to accept an individual challenge."

"Interesting," her mom said as she flagged the waitress down for more coffee. "So, what was your challenge Honey?"

"I'm glad you asked," Terry said, as she took a deep breath. "That's why I thought it was a good thing you came down this weekend."

"Oh, really," her mom looked up from the entree that she was enjoying.

Clearing her throat, Terry laid her napkin on the table. "Well, let me start by saying that I've noticed a real change in you this last month, and it's for the better, I might add."

"I'm so glad you have, because I've really tried to be a better mom. I know in the past I've been quite selfish, and preoccupied with myself, but I do love you Honey. I hope you know that?"

"Well, I've never felt that—that is until now, so I appreciate your effort."

"Anyway, as I was saying, for a long time, in fact, for almost twenty years I've had this one dream that I couldn't understand. Every morning I would wake up feeling like I was suffocating and seeing myself go down a long dark hole. I was even thinking about seeing a counselor to find out what it was about, but then I received my challenge and the questions about my dream were pretty much answered."

"How did that happen?" her mom looked intently at her.

"Well, it's hard to explain, but I found out something about myself that happened years ago."

"What was that?" her mom asked, more slowly this time.

"What do you think it might be?" Terry asked her mom point blank.

"I wouldn't even begin to guess," her mom looked at her intently.

"Mom, I hate to even talk about this in public. Perhaps we should finish this conversation at home?"

"Why? Now that you've started it, let's continue on, if you don't mind."

"Well, it was about a botched abortion that you had years ago."

With that news, her mom's face went white, and she grabbed the table. "What?" She said a little too loudly. "What in the world are you talking about?" Her face turned from white to crimson. "I had no such thing!"

Terry looked stunned for a minute. "Why, you most certainly did! That's what my challenge revealed."

"I don't care if your challenge revealed you were sent down by aliens from outer space. That never happened!"

Terry looked up to see the manager coming over to their table.

"Is everything all right? Is there something wrong with the food?"

"No, no," her mom interrupted. "We're so sorry. We didn't realize we were talking so loudly. If you don't mind giving me the bill, we are ready to leave," her mom said with a strained smile.

"Gladly," he said and motioned the waitress to come over.

"It's my treat," Terry said as she opened her purse.

"No, I'm going to pay tonight. After all, I invited you here, so I will take care of it."

Terry shrugged and excused herself to go to the lady's room while her mom paid the bill. "Well, that went smoothly," she murmured as she turned around to see her mom wiping her eyes with a tissue.

Chapter 41

Henry and Claire walked out into the gardens and admired all the colorful flowers that were in bloom. Claire reached down to smell one of the crimson roses. "So beautiful and peaceful isn't it?" she said.

"Yes," Henry said and smiled.

"What's wrong?" Claire stood up. "Something bothering you?"

"Well, I'm thinking that it's time to go."

"Really? I thought you wanted to stay a little longer with Marisa? I think she's coming around."

Henry smiled and looked off towards the gardens surrounding the stately house. "Well, it's time for you to get back to work, and to let Marisa have some space. I don't want to keep pushing her. I thank the Lord, Tom has forgiven me and wants me to come and see him and the girls—that's more than I could have wished for. So now I'm ready to go home."

Claire could see that, so she grabbed his hand and they continued walking for a while. "Well, if we must, then I'm ready too. But let's just enjoy this moment a little longer."

"Of course, anything for you," Henry reached down to touch her face. "You are so beautiful Claire. I can't believe you would be interested in an old man like me!"

"You are a wonderful man, Henry!" she squeezed his hand. "Why wouldn't I?"

Just then they both heard Marisa yelling for them.

"Dad, Claire, please hurry!" As they both ran into the parlor, they saw her lying on the floor her left leg contorted backwards, and they immediately knew she had broken it.

"Oh, no! What happened?" said Claire as she ran over to help her.

"I don't know. It happened so fast. I was watering my plants and somehow slipped on the floor. Please, Dad, call an ambulance or something."

"I'm calling 911 right now."

The paramedics arrived and began to assess the situation, asking all sorts of questions. They put a brace on her broken leg and lifted her up onto the stretcher. Claire covered her with a warm blanket and walked out to the ambulance with her. "Will you ride with me to the hospital? I don't want to be alone." Marisa looked at Claire.

"Sure, Honey. Let me get my coat and tell your father to follow us over."

Henry walked out and met Claire coming back in, "Does she want me to ride with her?" Henry asked.

"Well, she asked if I would, if that's OK? I thought you might follow us over in your car?"

"Sure, I'll go get my keys, and I'll call Tom and let him know too. Tell her I will be there in a few minutes!"

Unforeseen

Terry and her mom left the restaurant without speaking. As they walked into the lobby, she looked at her mom, who was staring straight ahead. "Mom, I'm sorry, I didn't mean to hurt you, but I've been praying about telling you this for some time now."

"I didn't realize that," her mom said, still not looking her way. "But you don't know the whole story" she turned to her. "I guess I should have told you, but I didn't know about the dream you had been having."

"I understand," Terry said, "can we go for a ride or just get some fresh air?"

"I'm fine," Margaret said. "In fact, I'm really tired all of a sudden. Maybe I'll just go up to my room."

Terry suddenly felt defeated. "Please Mom, can we go into the bar and just sit a while. I don't want to leave like this." Margaret nodded and walked into the lounge area. "So, what's the whole story then, if I may ask mom?"

Margaret looked out the bay window as if pondering what to say. "You're not my daughter. I adopted you," she said slowly.

"What?" Terry said a little too loudly. She looked around to see if anyone had heard them.

"Why don't we continue this in my suite?" her Mom said quietly. "That way we can have a cup of tea as well."

Terry nodded. As the elevator moved quickly up to the eighth floor, she turned to her Mom. "So, what's going on, mom, and why didn't you tell me I was adopted?"

"Like I said in the restaurant, there's more to the story than you realize. Would you like some tea?"

"No, I'm not thirsty, but go ahead and fix you some. I'm going to take my shoes off if you don't mind. My feet are killing me!"

"OK, I'll call room service then." With that Margaret turned away, and Terry stood there watching her walk across the room. She noticed a sadness that wasn't there just a few hours ago and secretly wished she hadn't brought this up after all.

Feeling hurt, and frustrated, she grabbed the scarf around her neck to take it off, and almost choked herself. She sat down on the edge of her couch and started to pray for guidance. As she finished, she looked up to see her mom standing at the end of the couch staring at her.

"What it is Mom?" Terry said quietly.

"I was just thinking about what an intelligent and beautiful woman you've turned out to be. I'm very proud of you, Honey."

Feeling surprised at this turn of emotions, Terry got up to take off her shoes. "Thanks, Mom, but I don't feel so pretty."

"Oh, but you are. When I first got you, you were so needy. I had to let you sleep with me almost every night, or you would keep crying. I couldn't bear to hear you wearing yourself out like that." As she sat down on the couch beside Terry, she brushed her bangs back and grabbed her hand. "Honey, I loved you then, and I still love you today so much."

"Then why didn't I ever feel that love?" Terry looked into her mom's eyes? "I always felt disapproval from you and thought you couldn't wait for me to get out of the house."

"That wasn't the case at all," her mom said sadly. "When your dad left, I felt abandoned and rejected. I guess I took out my hurt and anger on you, and for that I am so sorry. Perhaps I blamed you secretly ... and that was wrong of me, because it had nothing to do with you."

"So, Mom, tell me about my adoption and my parents."

Just then room service rang the bell and came in with a beautiful china tea service, along with a big pot of steaming water. Margaret began to fix two cups of tea. "Honey, what I'm going to tell you might be a bit of a shock, but I'm going to be as accurate as I can."

"I'm not sure if I could be shocked any more than I am right now, but please go ahead," Terry nodded.

"Your Aunt Helen was very young when she met a boy at her church. He was the pastor's son, and they started to date. The pastor and his family were very strict and always chaperoned their dates. That was until the senior prom. Somehow, they let them both go alone, and one thing led to another, and Helen got pregnant. Since she was my younger sister, she confided in me, and no one else. When she was further along in her pregnancy, we knew she would need to tell our parents.

So, one evening after dad came home from work, we sat down and told them together. They were devastated, of course, and immediately called up our grandmother and arranged to have Helen go stay with her until she delivered. But that night Helen slipped out of the house and ran away. We searched and searched for her. Then I found out that she had gone to stay with a girlfriend." Margaret paused to see if Terry wanted her to continue.

"Go on," Terry sat there hardly moving.

"Anyway, her friend told her to have an abortion. Said it would be quick and easy, and she could go on with her life as if nothing had happened. Except that's not the way things went. Deciding to listen to her and not wanting to go to her grandmother's, she went to the clinic the next day. It turned out that when she got there, they rushed her into making a decision and started the procedure without even giving her time to think about it.

When she woke up she saw blood everywhere and began to scream. A woman came in and told her to shut up, and that everything would be all right, but Helen kept screaming and saying, 'Where's my baby, tell me where's my baby?'

Soon the doctor came in and tried to give her a sedative, but she knocked it out of his hand, and this time they told her the baby was dead. She was devastated and was never the same after that. Oh, she went home and finished school, but left shortly after graduation and was never heard from again. I tried looking for her for years after that, but never had any success."

Quietly Terry asked the question that had been pounding in her head since her mom started talking. "So, was I the baby?"

"Yes," Margaret looked up.

"And they told her I was dead?"

"Yes," her mom nodded taking another sip of tea.

"What happened with the procedure they did on her?"

Margaret wiped a tear from her eye and continued on. "Well, one of the other workers there saw the nurse trying to suffocate you in the room next door, but when she heard Helen screaming, they left you lying there on the table, and tried to calm her down. When they came back to the room, you were gone."

"What?" Terry was sitting on the edge of her seat.

"Apparently Helen's friend heard the commotion and tried to get into the room where Helen was, but she accidentally stumbled upon you, with a pillow lying on your face. Mortified, she started giving you mouth to mouth until you finally took a deep breath and started to cry. When you whimpered, she picked you up and ran out of the clinic."

Stunned, Terry just sat there trying to take it all in. "Wow, she saved my life then?"

"Yes, she did, but she didn't have the nerve to bring the baby back to Helen. So, she kept you and told her parents she had found you."

"Did they believe that?"

"Well, they were older and thought that perhaps it was hers, and that she was lying to them. But they loved you as their own. Then one day she came to our house to find Helen, but we told her she had left, and we didn't know where she was. That's when she broke down and told us what had happened that day.

"We all were shocked, but I was so relieved she had saved you, that I asked right then and there to take you. My parents weren't happy about it. At that time, I was engaged, so when Ted and I got married, we took you as our own. At first, he seemed excited about being an instant Dad, but then he got laid off from his job and we began to have money problems. So, one thing led to another, and one day he just walked out and never came back."

"I see," Terry said and got up to open the door that lead to the terrace. "I think I need some fresh air."

"Are you all right?" her Mom asked.

"I guess—just trying to let it all sink in, that's all."

"I know that's a lot to absorb all at once, but you needed the whole story."

"Yes, but it doesn't make it any easier to hear."

"No, I imagine it doesn't, but I wanted you to know that I've always loved you."

"I see that now, and I'm grateful. I really am … it's just hard."

Margaret got up and hugged her, saying nothing.

"Thanks Mom, and I'm sorry I accused you without knowing the whole story."

"That's all right honey, I would have done the same thing. I guess I was shocked, and I hoped that this day would never come. But now that it has, at least the truth is out and that will set us both free."

"Yes," Terry replied, her eyes glistening with tears. "Yes, it will."

Victoria Lynn Deviney

Chapter 42

"I hope she's not in too much pain," Claire said, looking up at Henry.

"Me too, Honey, me too," Henry said, as he patted her hand. "She'll be all right, she's a tough one," he smiled.

"So, I guess this means we're going to be here a little longer?" Claire said.

"Well, let's just take it one step at a time," Henry sighed. "You need to get back to work, and I still have one more meeting if I'm counting correctly."

"Yes, we missed last week. We really need to be there for the final one," Claire replied.

"I bet she'll be able to come home today, knowing Marisa," Henry smiled. "She does have help available who will wait on her hand and foot—no pun intended." Claire laughed, and hit Henry's arm.

"I can get you on a flight home tomorrow if I need to stay a few extra days. But I should be able to make the last meeting regardless," Henry added. Just then Henry heard his name being called. "That's me," he stood up and shook the doctor's hand. "So, how is she?"

"Well, it looks like it's a clean break, so no need for surgery. But she will be in a cast for at least 12 weeks, then a boot for a few weeks more. But if there are no other complications, I think her leg will be even stronger after it heals. She will just need to slow down, and I have a feeling that might be a challenge for her," he grinned.

"You're right about that," Henry smiled. "But, she does have people who will be able to assist her, so I feel confident they will make her slow down a little."

"Will you be staying for a while?" the doctor asked.

"Claire and I were planning to leave first thing in the morning, unless you feel I'm needed here?"

"That's your call. I can't make that decision for you. Why don't you ask Marisa?"

"OK," Henry looked over to Claire.

"Well, she should be out in a moment, she's just finishing up in triage. I've already spoken to her about slowing down, so hopefully she will listen."

After he left, Henry sat back down, and Claire put his hand in hers. "It will be fine," she said.

"Sure, just a little disappointed. It's not that I don't want to stay, it's just that I felt the Lord prodding me to leave tomorrow."

"Well, if I were you, I would just ask Marisa straight out if she wants you to stay a little longer. And if she's insists you leave, then leave, and come back in a few weeks to check on her."

"That's a good idea," Henry replied as he looked up to see Marisa coming through the door in a wheelchair.

"Well, look who is all fixed up," Henry grinned and took hold of Marisa's hand.

"Yes, well, who would have guessed I would have broken my leg, and right when y'all are leaving." Marisa replied.

Unforeseen

"Well, Honey, that's what I wanted to ask you. Claire needs to get back to work, but if you want me to stay a few days longer, I can. Just tell me what you would like me to do."

"Thanks Dad for asking, but I'll be fine. Michael will be over this afternoon, and I've got my maid and groundskeeper there if I need anything."

"Then how about if I come back down to see you in a couple of weeks?" Henry asked.

"That's fine. I'm not going anywhere for a while," Marisa looked around impatiently. "I'm ready to go, let's get out of here," she looked up at the nurse who was pushing her. "Can you get my crutches, Dad?"

Henry grabbed them as he and Claire walked out with Marisa, who was already ordering the poor nurse around like one of her assistants.

Trent stepped into his office. Already tired before the day had started, he sat down to turn on his computer. Glancing over at his calendar, he saw several events scheduled for the week. Thinking he just didn't have it in him to do this anymore, suddenly his phone rang, and he jumped to grab it. "Good morning, Pastor Jeff. How are you?"

"Fine Son, just checking to see if you're available to meet for lunch today?"

"Sure, I just got into the office, probably will work until late tonight."

"OK, I'll come by, and we'll go out somewhere close if that's all right with you?"

"That's great," but as he hung up the phone, he had an uneasiness come over him like a dark cloud right before a storm.

Trent didn't even notice when the door opened, and the pastor stepped in. "Am I disturbing you?" Pastor Jeff smiled.

"Oh, Pastor, I didn't hear you come in! I was trying to decide which games to use for the youth retreat!"

"What time is it?" Trent asked as he shut down his computer.

"It's 12:30, Son. Sorry I'm a little late, I had a phone call I needed to take."

"No problem," Trent replied as they walked out of the office.

"I thought we would go to that little Mexican restaurant up the street," Pastor said. "I've heard good things about it," as they got into his car.

"Sounds good, I'm starving. I didn't have breakfast this morning, I was late taking Jacob to the sitters."

"How is Maggie doing?" Pastor Rob asked as he pulled out of the church parking lot.

"Oh, she's doing great," Trent grinned. "Dr. Nelson said if things go as planned, she might be able to come home week after next!"

"Oh, how wonderful. I'm sure Jacob and you can't wait!"

"No, we're ready to have things back to normal—well, as normal as they can be right now."

"I understand," Pastor Jeff said. As they sat down in a booth towards the back, both looked at the specials and ordered the same thing. "Looks like we're creatures of habit, aren't we?" Pastor Jeff laughed.

"Yes. Well, you just can't go to wrong with fajitas," Trent laughed.

"You're right," pastor said, as he dug into the chips and salsa.

"So," Trent said slowly, "is everything all right, Pastor? I mean, we haven't gone out to eat together since I came on staff several years ago."

Unforeseen

"I just wanted to speak to you privately about what the board decided last week concerning your six-month sabbatical."

"Oh, I see," Trent said fidgeting a little.

Pastor Jeff looked intently into Trent's eyes, and continued, "After much deliberation, they just thought it unwise to let you go away that long with pay. But they did say you could take three months off without pay, if you still thought you needed this time."

Disappointed, Trent breathed a sigh of relief for at least not being let go. "Well, even though I am disappointed, I appreciate them at least discussing and voting on it."

"Trent, you're a great youth minister, and we don't want to lose you. It's just that the church can't afford to pay you if you're not there. I do hope you understand," Pastor Jeff spoke softly.

"I do," Trent smiled.

"I sure hope this won't affect your inheritance in any way," the Pastor continued.

"I don't think it will. All they said was that I should take a step of faith and ask. But, I have a meeting tomorrow morning, so I will find out then," Trent replied. They both looked up to see the food on its way to their table.

Chapter 43

After being on the road for two weeks, Claire couldn't wait to see everyone and catch up with them. She looked up from her computer and saw Henry watching her quietly. "Hey there, I didn't hear you walk in," she smiled as she continued filling out her weekly calendar. "Is there anyone else here yet?"

"No, just me for now. I came in a little early to see you."

"Oh, really. How did you sleep last night?" Claire asked.

"Like a baby," Henry grinned. "It was good to be back in my own bed."

"I know what you mean. I have fun traveling, but I'm always ready to come back home."

"Well, I appreciate you so much for being such a good sport and going with me," Henry grinned.

"It was my pleasure, and I'm glad you asked me!"

Just then Trent peeked in, "Hey there! So glad to have you both back in town!"

"Trent, it's good to see you!" Henry grabbed him and gave him a big hug.

"How is Maggie doing?" Claire asked.

"Oh, she's doing great. I think she'll be able to come home from rehab next week!"

"That's good to hear!" Henry replied. "So, do you have anyone to help you with everything once you get her home?"

"Well, you wouldn't believe it, but Margaret is!"

"Wow!" both Claire and Henry said at the same time. "So, things have been happening while we were gone!" Henry added.

"Yes, a lot! But I'm sure you'll hear it all when everyone gets here."

"I better get the coffee made," Claire chuckled. "I almost forgot, I've been away so long!"

"So, Trent, tell me how you're holding up?" Henry asked after Claire left the room.

"I'm doing pretty good. I had lunch with my Pastor yesterday. He told me some disappointing news."

"What's that?" Henry asked concerned.

"Oh, he said the board voted not to pay me for a six-month sabbatical. That I could take off three months without pay, if I felt I needed to. But that's all they could give me."

"So, what do you think about that?" Henry replied.

"Well, I asked, and that's all the challenge said to do. I'm not in control of what the answer is."

"You're right," Henry smiled, "that's all you can do. That's what I did as well. I tried to make amends with my children—it was bittersweet though. Of course, the saddest thing for me was to find out my middle son, David, had passed away of a drug overdose a year ago."

"Oh, I'm so sorry to hear that," Trent responded.

"Well, it caused me to have a mild heart attack, I was in the hospital for a couple of days."

"Oh no, Henry! Why didn't you call me?"

"Nonsense, Claire was with me very step of the way. I woke up the next morning to see her sitting right there beside me, she had stayed all night."

"That's great," Trent smiled, "it was a good thing she went with you after all. Listen, I'm praying about some things, and I know the Lord will direct me when the right time comes, but I appreciate your prayers too."

"I certainly will," Henry patted Trent on the back. "Come on, why don't we get us a cup of coffee before the women come?"

"Sure, I'm ready for one," Trent said, as they walked across to where Claire was putting things together. Just then Margaret and Terry came walking in.

"Why, everyone's back!" they smiled and hugged both Claire and Henry.

"It's so good seeing you all again," Henry said. "It seems like a long time!"

"Two weeks does makes a difference, doesn't it?" Claire laughed. "I still can't believe this is the last meeting," she said and looked over at Henry. "By the way, did you all meet with Mr. Simpson last week?"

"Yes, he was very cordial," Terry laughed. "Said we could either accept the money or pass it on to the next group."

"That's right," Margaret added. "Apparently this so called "inheritance" is more about our challenges than it is about the money."

Claire nodded and said, "Indeed it is. I hope you all realize what a gift you've each been given. Not many people get a second chance to have a 'do over' in life."

Everyone quietly pondered this. Glancing around, Claire noticed Henry smiling at her, and suddenly felt her heart beat wildly. "And," Claire continued, "I hope each of you will continue to keep in touch with one another after all is said and done. I know the group before you has, for the most part!"

"Oh, we plan on it," Trent spoke up, and they all agreed!

"Well, I have quite a bit of news," Margaret smiled. "First, the Lord opened up a door for me to help Maggie when she comes home, and I'm so grateful for that."

"We are too!" Trent said, and smiled.

"However, my challenge, as you all know, was to forgive my ex-husband for his infidelity. And you won't believe what happened last week?"

"What?" Henry spoke first.

"Well, I accidentally ran into him at the hospital while I was visiting Maggie."

"Really," Trent said, "what happened?"

"Yes, tell us what happened!" Terry spoke up.

"Well, he was there to pick up his wife, who just had a baby, and we both rode the same elevator up. Somehow, I apologized, which led him to do the same and at the end, he hugged me and said he was going to send me a check from the assets of the divorce—that I deserved it!"

"Wow," they all said at once, "That's amazing."

"Yes, it is, it felt like a weight lifted off me, and I sure can use the extra money."

Laughing they all agreed.

"I found out some very interesting news from my mom as well," Terry spoke up.

"Do tell!" Claire said.

"She came up to see me this past weekend. So, I met her for dinner and brought it up then. She was so upset that we kinda made a scene at the restaurant. I thought they were going to ask us to leave. But we quit talking about it until we got back to her hotel room. Anyway, it seems that not only was I almost aborted, but I was also adopted by my mom!"

"What!" Henry said, and you could hear a pin drop.

"Yes," Terry nodded her head. "mom's sister was the one who was pregnant with me and tried to abort me. To make a long story short, after the botched abortion, she ran away, and Mom, who was already engaged to my dad, decided to raise me as her own."

"Wow," Trent said. "That's a strange turn of events. You sure can't make something like that up, can you?"

"No, you can't," Terry frowned. "Anyway, she apologized for not telling me sooner."

"That's truly amazing the way God revealed it all at just the right time, don't you think?" Margaret replied.

"Yes, I have to agree," Terry said. "God is good, isn't He?"

"Well, seems like you both have also completed your challenges," Henry grinned. "I've pretty much completed mine as far as contacting my children and making amends as well. Tom, my oldest son immediately forgave me, but my youngest daughter Marisa is a little harder to get to. But at least she's letting me into her life."

"So that leaves me," Trent said, as they looked over at him. "As you all know, my challenge has been a 'challenge'" he said laughing. "I kinda knew it would be a miracle if the church would let me have a six-month paid sabbatical. So yesterday, at lunch, the Pastor told me the deacons turned that request down. Instead they said if I needed one, I could take a three-month leave without pay. So, needless to say, that was a little disappointing."

But one thing I haven't told all of you is that I believe God may be leading me in another direction anyway. It all started when Maggie was hospitalized, and every day I would walk down the hall, just to get a little exercise. I started to look into the rooms of those who were sick, and God began to prompt me to pray for them, and for their families.

Well, last week as I was doing this, again I felt a my heart leap. It was as if God let me know that He was changing directions for

Unforeseen

my life and ministry. I'm not sure what all this means yet, but I'm excited to see how it all turns out!"

"Well," Henry responded. "Sounds like the Lord is stirring your nest. It does say in the Bible, 'He uses all things for His good.'"

"You're right," Trent nodded. "So even though I won't be getting a sabbatical, perhaps the accident Maggie had was for a reason. Though I wished it had been me instead of her."

"We understand," Terry spoke up, "but just like my news—somehow, after I confronted it, God has brought something good out of it. My mom and I are getting closer for the first time."

"I can see that," Margaret said quietly. "Through the pain of my divorce and all the mistakes I have made in my life ... well, God is redeeming it, and not only that, I have a whole new future ahead of me!"

Henry sat there quietly listening to each person share what God had done and was doing in their lives Suddenly he knew what he needed to do, and he wasn't going to waste another day. Looking over to Trent, he whispered something in this ear. Trent grinned and nodded his head, and Henry breathed a sigh of relief. *Thank you, Lord. Thank you for letting me know* he said silently.

Chapter 44

Trent pulled up to Henry's house and honked the horn. Henry looked out and waved while putting on his coat. Quickly checking to see if he had his wallet, he closed the door behind him and walked to the car.

"Hey there! Trent smiled, are you ready to go and spend some money?"

"Absolutely," Henry said, and grinned. "In fact, I'm pretty excited too!"

"Well, all right then," Trent grinned, "I've called a friend of mine, who is a jeweler, and he has some rings already picked out for you."

"Thank you" Henry said. "Doesn't hurt to have a game-plan does it?"

"By the way, have you said anything about this to Claire yet?"

"No, not a thing. But I've asked her out for dinner tomorrow night."

"Are you nervous?" Trent looked over at Henry, who was gazing out the window.

Unforeseen

"Just a little, but I believe the Lord has worked all of this out, and whatever she says will be all right with me."

"Wow, I wish I could feel like that when I'm taking a risk. I get all caught up in wanting my own way. Sometimes, it's hard to trust God and leave it in His hands."

"I understand, Son. I guess this comes from experience, and age mostly. So many times in the past, I made it happen all by myself, only to find I was unfulfilled and discontented afterwards. Since giving my life to Christ, I found out that it's better to have what He wants me to have than to find out later I made a colossal mistake."

Trent looked over at Henry. "You're right. Every time I've waited on the Lord, I've never regretted it."

With that they turned into the shopping center, and Henry asked, "Can we pray together for the right choice on rings?"

"Sure," Trent said, and grabbed Henry's outstretched hand. As they both sat there praying, they could feel a peace that God was indeed smiling down on them.

Staring off into space, Claire rolled her pen in her hand, wondering what this fancy dinner was all about. Henry seemed to be a little vague in telling her too many details. He just wanted to take her out for a nice meal to thank her for coming along with him on his adventure.

"I suppose that's all there is to it," she said to herself. But something in her spirit had her thinking otherwise. Suddenly, looking up, she noticed Martha at the door. "Oh hello! Sorry my mind was a thousand miles away. How long have you been standing there?"

"Not long, I didn't want to disturb you. You looked like you were trying to figure something out," Martha smiled.

"No, no. Come on in. Just getting some paperwork finished. How can I help you?" Claire asked, as she walked over to the coffee pot. "Would you like some coffee?"

"Sure, why not?" Martha answered, and sat down in the chair.

"You look tired," Claire said, as she looked over her shoulder at Martha.

"Well, I'm moving out of Terry's house. I found a little one-bedroom apartment close to Trent and Maggie's neighborhood. Thought I should be close, just in case they needed me."

"That's nice," Claire gave Martha her coffee.

"Will Trent and Maggie be paying you?"

"Oh yes. It's quite generous. But I'm not sure what he's going to do about his job. So that makes me a little nervous."

"I see," Claire leaned forward. "Do you think he's going to take his three-month sabbatical?"

"Perhaps, or maybe even take another job, the way Maggie talked the other day."

"Really? Where?" Claire asked.

"I'm not sure. Maggie just indicated they've been praying about some decisions."

"Oh," Claire nodded. "Well, I hope you'll be able to stay with them at least a year until you can get back on your feet."

"Me too. I've never been in a situation like this. I've always had good jobs and a good financial standing."

"I understand," Claire smiled, "but it appears that the Lord is taking care of you, especially since your ex-husband is going to give you a part of the assets you both acquired. So, I believe this is just something God is taking you through to draw you closer to Himself."

"You think so?" Martha asked.

"Oh yes. Everything we go through in life will either draw us closer, or lead us away, from the Lord. It's all in how we choose to respond to the circumstances and situations."

"Um," Martha said thoughtfully, "well, I hope I am responding well. I want to—it's just that I get anxious at times."

"I understand that completely. We are human after all," Claire said thoughtfully. "God knows our heart, and that's all that matters."

"Well, I'll let you get back to work. Thanks for your time," Martha said, as she got up to go.

"You're so welcome, and congratulations on your new place!"

"Thanks," Martha smiled. As she walked out, Claire prayed for her and also for her newfound faith.

"Beautiful," was all Henry could say, "just beautiful. This is perfect for Claire—elegant but not pretentious." They both agreed, and the sale was complete. Afterwards they went for a nice lunch and reminisced about all that had happened since they started meeting together.

"Henry," Trent said, putting his fork down. "I've got something that Maggie and I have been discussing and praying about. I want to get your opinion too."

"Sure," Henry stopped eating.

"Well, I told you all that I believe God is changing my ministry direction."

"Yes," Henry acknowledged.

"Well, I've been having a strong desire to pursue a chaplaincy at one of the hospitals in town."

"I think that's great Trent. You would be such a blessing to so many people. I've watched you pray and care for Maggie, and with Terry, and Martha, too. You're a compassionate and kind man that could help people, who are going through tragedy and suffering. Does this mean you're not going to pursue the sabbatical then?"

"Since the Lord is leading me in this direction, I believe I've got my answer about that now."

Henry nodded in agreement, "Yes, sometimes people get the ball rolling, but it's God who makes the moves! Do you know what the first step towards this new calling will be?"

"Well, first I'll apply for a position of chaplaincy, and I'll just keep working at the church until I hear. Then perhaps I can keep working while I'm training, until the time comes when I need to quit. That way, we won't stop getting a paycheck."

"I think that's very wise of you, Trent, and if you need any help financially, you know where I am," he winked.

"Thank you, Henry," Trent smiled. As they got ready to leave, he reached over and took the ticket. "I'm paying for this. Just wanted to say how much I've appreciated your friendship over the past few weeks."

"Why, thank you," Henry replied, "I feel the same way. No amount of inheritance could pay for our time together, that's for sure!"

Chapter 45

The restaurant was already crowded by the time they sat down to eat, and Henry was a little distracted.

"Honey, is everything alright?" Claire asked as she put her napkin on her lap.

"Oh, yes. I was just hoping the restaurant would be a little quieter tonight, but it is Friday, isn't it?" he laughed.

"Yes," Claire smiled, "unfortunately a lot of people go out on the weekends."

As the waiter came up to get their drink order, Henry looked over to see the man at the piano nodding to him. Excusing himself he went to the bathroom, stopping briefly to give the man a tip. Smiling, the man slipped it behind the sheet of music.

Claire was looking over the menu when he returned. "What are you in the mood for Honey?"

"I think I'm in the mood for a good steak!" he said, grinning.

"I haven't had a steak in a long time," Claire nodded. "That sounds good to me!" Claire sat with her hands crossed on the table, "just what are we celebrating tonight?"

"Well. Whatever do you mean?" Henry replied vaguely.

"Well, this is the most popular restaurant in the city, and I know it's not cheap!"

"Are you calling me a cheapskate?" Henry chuckled.

"No," Claire laughed, "I really appreciate you bringing me here, but there was no need to thank me, I so enjoyed my vacation with you and your children."

"I just wanted to wine and dine you tonight. After all, almost every time we've eaten together, you've cooked! So just thought you might enjoy being waited on."

"As a matter of fact, I do," Claire smiled, "so thank you for your thoughtfulness!"

"You're very welcome," Henry said and looked over to the man playing the piano. With that the man suddenly played a drum roll, and everyone looked up.

Henry was already on his knees beside Claire with ring in hand when she realized what was going on. Turning beet red, she stammered something unintelligible but seemed to nod 'yes' as he slipped the ring on her finger. Everyone clapped as the pianist began playing a romantic song that Henry had picked out. Before Claire could say anything, she was being escorted out onto the dance floor.

"Why Henry. I'm speechless!" Claire finally said as they continued to dance. "You took me by surprise!"

"That was the idea," he laughed. "You are going to marry me, aren't you?"

Claire, pretending to ponder the question, answered, "Of course, My Dear!"

"Great! Since we aren't getting any younger, let's get married right away!" he added.

"Henry, my head is already spinning. Let me catch my breath, and then let's talk about a date."

"I guess I'm a little impatient, now that I've found a beautiful and godly woman!"

Claire blushed and said, "Thank you," quietly. The rest of the evening they talked about the wedding, and the unusual turn of events that had led them together.

Trent looked up to see Maggie being wheeled into the room. "You look tired," he said, as they put her back into the bed.

"Oh, nothing more than usual," she smiled. "They do make you sweat, but that's a good thing! Hopefully in another couple of weeks I can come home!"

"I sure hope so," Trent smiled. "It's already been way too long, hasn't it?"

"Sure has," Maggie commented. "Honey, I'm hungry for a big juicy hamburger. I've been thinking about one all day!"

"Well, your wish is my command!" he said.

"Thanks, Sweetie. I really appreciate all you've done for me since I've been in here."

"You would have done the same for me, and probably been a little better at it too," he laughed.

As Maggie began combing her hair, she looked over at Trent, "So, what's on your mind?"

"What do you mean?" Trent said.

"You know what I mean," she smiled.

"You know me so well, don't you?" Trent sat up straighter.

"Of course, I do Sweetie. That's what a wife's job is. She studies her man and asks the Lord for wisdom and discernment to help him when she can!"

"Really?" Trent replied. "Do all women do this, or just you?"

Maggie smiled, "So tell me what's going on?" she said, as she laid back on her pillow and closed her eyes.

"Well, I think I've gotten my answer about the chaplaincy, and I'm ready to start the process."

She opened her eyes and smiled. "Yeah! I'm so glad you've gotten confirmation. I've been praying intently since we first talked about it."

Trent looked relieved. "Well, I will probably have to go back to school and get some training, but I think I can do that while I'm still working at the church. That way, I can start applying to some hospitals now, and still keep my job."

"It sounds like you've got a plan, Honey. Are you sure it won't be too much on you?"

"No, in fact, I'm kind of excited about this change."

"I'll be home soon, and Martha will be helping me, which will free you up a little more."

"I know that. I wouldn't have even thought about doing this kind of work, had I not been here with you."

"So, God does work all things out for our good, doesn't He?" Maggie smiled and grabbed his hand.

"He sure does, Honey. He sure does."

Claire was quiet as Henry pulled out onto the freeway. "Are you, all right?" Henry said.

"Oh yes. I'm just trying to decide on where to have our wedding, and who all to invite."

Henry smiled, "I will leave all those details up to you. I'm not sure about that stuff."

"Oh no, you don't! You're not getting out of it that easy," she laughed! "In fact, I'm going to need your help with everything," she said, as she touched his hand.

"OK, I got it," Henry grinned, as he turned into her neighborhood.

"In fact," Claire said, "I would love to have the first inheritance group to attend my wedding, it would be a wonderful way for everyone to meet."

"Yes, it would," Henry replied. "Tom said they were a great group of people."

Claire patted his hand. "Yes, I think this would be a great way to get us all together."

Chapter 46

Wedding plans were under way as Claire busied herself with the invitations. Meanwhile, Terry found a beautiful venue for the reception, and Martha was coordinating the actual ceremony at Claire's church.

Henry reached for his cell phone that morning and dialed Tom's number. "Good morning, Son!"

"Hey Dad, how are the wedding plans going?"

"Well, Son, you know how it is—you get a bunch of women together and soon you are left in the dust."

Laughing, Tom agreed, "So what can I do to help?"

"Well, would you bless me by being my best man? And having the girls be the little flower attendants?"

"Oh, they would love that. And I would be honored too."

"Have you spoken to Marisa about coming?" Henry asked.

"I left a message with the housekeeper, who said she was out of town. Apparently, even with her cast, she is still working like crazy."

"That's Marisa for you," Henry chuckled, "She doesn't let anything get her down for too long does she? "I do hope she can take time off to come, and at least be a part of this day," he added.

"That would be nice for sure. Listen, Dad, the girls and I are going to have dinner with her this weekend when she gets back from her trip, so I will put a good word in for you!"

"Thanks, Son. I would appreciate that! Well, better get back to planning the honeymoon!"

"Oh, where are you two going?" Tom asked.

"I was thinking it might be nice to go to the mountains, so I was looking at Denver, maybe a ski lodge," Henry responded.

"Do you two ski, Dad? I mean do you think that's safe?"

"Well, for an old man I'm a pretty good skier," he said chucking. "But there's other fun things to do there as well."

"It's a beautiful time of year to go, for sure. Whatever you do, it will be fun," Tom replied.

"Come to think of it, Tom, I know it hasn't been easy for you this past year with Katy being gone. Have you ever thought about dating again?"

There was a long silence before Tom spoke up, "Dad, it's just too early. It's only been a little over a year now, and I'm not ready to join the dating scene yet."

"I understand. I didn't mean to pry, but you are such a good man and still so young; it was just a thought."

"Thanks, Dad, but that's not where I am, maybe one day."

"Yes, maybe so, Son. Well, I will let you go. Thanks for agreeing to be my best man!"

"Hey, thanks for asking, and I will call you after I speak to Marisa," Tom added.

"OK, see you soon," as Henry hung up the phone he had a tug in his spirit to ask Claire if Terry could be a part of the wedding too.

Claire looked up Matthew's international number and preceded to dial hoping that he was home, and available. "Matthew, is that you?" Claire asked excitedly.

"Yes, Claire. I can't believe it's you!"

"I know," Claire replied, "it's so good to hear your voice! How's Sandy?"

"Oh, she's great. She's taking care of little Emma right now."

"Oh my. You have a little girl?"

"Yes, we just had her a few months ago. She's the apple of my eye!" Matthew said laughing. "She's already got me wrapped around her little finger!"

"I bet so. You all must be so excited!"

"Yes, we all are, especially Sandy's parents—they love babysitting."

"Well, the reason I'm calling is that I've got some good news too, I'm getting married!"

"Congratulations!" Matthew immediately responded.

"That's why I'm calling, to see is if you all could come to the wedding. I'm marrying a man that I met through the inheritance group that was chosen this year. He's a wonderful gentleman, and it would be a blessing for all of you from the first inheritance group to meet Henry. In fact, Henry is the father of Tom, Katie's husband".

"Wow!" Matthew replied. "that's a God thing isn't it? Well, I can't promise you that we'll be able to make it, but we sure will try. We hardly get back to the States anymore. In fact, we haven't been there since Katie's funeral, if you can believe that!"

"Well, then, maybe it's time to come home!" Claire replied.

"Maybe so," Matthew said. "I'll talk to Sandy about it, and get back to you via email, if that's OK?"

"Sure," Claire responded. "Please give Sandy my love, and a big hug for little Emma!"

"Will do," Matthew said. As he put the phone down, he had a feeling that this may be just the thing Sandy needed to lift her spirits since the birth of little Emma.

Claire then called Nicole and was told that she was currently out of the office. Leaving a message, she silently prayed for her protection and strength as well. Lastly, she contacted Clay, who answered the phone on the first ring. "Clay Henderson, how can I help you?" he said.

"Clay, it's Claire from the inheritance group."

"Claire, how in the world are you?"

"Well, actually I'm doing well. In fact, I'm getting married!"

"Congratulations! So, who's the lucky guy?"

"Well, it's a man who was in our inheritance group this year."

"How interesting," Clay replied.

"So how are you doing, Clay?"

"I couldn't be better. I just got married myself, a little over four months ago now. I married that wonderful nurse I met when dad was hospitalized."

"Congratulations, I thought that she just might be the one for you! I remembered you speaking about her. The reason I'm calling is to see if you both would be able to come to my wedding? In fact, I just spoke to Matthew who is overseas, and would you believe that they just had a baby, a few months ago?"

"Yes, that's what I heard! I try to keep up with him via email. Do you think they will come?" Clay asked.

"Well, I hope so. But it is a long distance and expensive, so we'll see."

Clay made a note to contact Matthew and ask if he could help out a little with the trip should he want to come.

"Well, Melissa and I would be honored to come to your wedding. Thanks so much for asking us! Just let us know the time and place!"

"I'm trying to get the invitations with all the details out this week. But it's going to be in three weeks at my church!"

"Then we will see you there!" Clay said. "If you need anything beforehand, just give us a shout."

Claire hung up the phone elated. "It's been way too long," she whispered, "way too long." As she started out of the office, her phone rang. "Hello," she said quickly.

"Claire, it's Robin, Nicole's assistant. I just received your message and wanted to get back to you."

"Oh, Robin, thanks. I just wanted to speak to Nicole when she has time. I know she's busy."

With that Robin interrupted. "Claire, Nicole is at home."

"Oh, I thought the lady said she was out of the office." Claire responded.

"Well, she's very sick. She's just found out that her cancer has come back."

Silent, Claire just sat there for a moment, gathering her thoughts. "Oh, I am so sorry to hear that. I had no idea. I wish I would have known sooner."

"Well, it all happened so fast, it's only been a few weeks. She started noticing she was tired a lot, but just thought it was the nature of the job. Then she started forgetting things. So, she went in to have a PET scan, and they found the cancer had spread to her brain." Robin explained.

"Oh my. So, what is the prognosis?" Claire asked slowly.

"Well, they said it could be a few months to a year at the most."

"Is it OK if I call her?" Claire asked.

"Sure, do you have her number?"

"Yes, I will just give her a quick call. And thanks so much, Robin, for letting me know." Suddenly the excitement she had, turned to grief, as she thought about losing another wonderful lady and friend in the inheritance group. As Claire picked the phone up to call Nicole, she silently prayed for the right words to say.

"Hello?" she immediately recognized Nicole's cheerful voice.

"Nicole, it's Claire from the inheritance group!"

"Claire, how nice to hear you. What a surprise!"

"Yes, I know. It's been way too long, hasn't it?" Claire responded.

"So, how are you doing?" Nicole asked.

"I'm wonderful. In fact, that's why I'm calling you. I'm getting married if you can believe that!"

"Why, of course I can. You are a very attractive lady!" Nicole laughed.

"You're too sweet! But I'm not exactly young anymore."

"One can never be too old for love," Nicole laughed.

"I called your office, but Robin called me back and told me your news, Nicole."

"You mean about my cancer?"

"Yes, I hope that was all right?" Claire asked.

"Oh, yes. It's been a shock for all of us, but the Lord healed me before, and so we are counting on His mercy again."

"I will be praying for you all too. If there's anything I can do for you, please let me know."

"Thank you, Claire. I'm just resting this week. The doctors are trying a new experimental drug on me, and it's made me a little weak. But I will be back in the office next week working part time, at least. They can't keep me away, I just love what I'm doing!"

"That's wonderful," Claire shook her head. "The Lord works in mysterious ways, doesn't He?"

"Yes, He sure does. And believe me, I'm planning on working a long time, regardless of what the doctors say!"

"Well, both Henry and I will stand with you on that!" Claire said. "Anyway, if you feel like it, we would love to have you and your family be a part of this wonderful celebration."

"I wouldn't miss it," Nicole said. "Just let me know the details."

"I will be sending out the invitations this week, so, you will get one in the mail by next week, for sure."

"Will everyone else be coming too?" Nicole asked.

"I know Clay and his new wife are coming."

"He's married?" Nicole interrupted.

"Oh, yes. He married that nurse, Melissa. The one who helped his dad in the hospital!"

"That's great!" Nicole said. "I hate that we've not kept in touch like we said we were going to do."

"Well, maybe the wedding will help," Claire replied.

"I've kept up better with Matthew, and I know he's so excited to have a family now. That little Emma is so cute!" Nicole replied.

"I just heard the news from him today," Claire laughed. "I hope they all are able to come too!"

"It will be fun to enjoy a wedding this time, instead of a funeral, for sure," Nicole added.

"Yes, it will," Claire replied. "It was so good to catch up with you, Nicole, and I can't wait to see you, Rob, and the girls!"

"Thanks, we can't wait to see everyone and to meet the lucky man who got you!"

"Thank you," Claire said softly. "I can't wait for him to meet all of you as well!"

"See you soon, bride-to-be!" Nicole said. As she hung up, she thanked the Lord for reconnecting them all, once again.

Chapter 47

Claire woke up early. Turning over, she saw that it was only 6:45am. She smiled, realizing that in just a few hours' time she would be married! She yawned and stretched, thinking about how after so many years of watching others' lives change, hers was now changing too. "Thank you, Lord," she whispered, "for giving me another opportunity to love someone again."

Mentally she went over all the details and thought about little Emma, Matthew and Sandy flying, even now, to get there. Just as she was going over the order of service, the phone rang. "Hello?" she said, sitting up a little too fast.

"Hello Beautiful!" Henry said.

"Well, you're up early, and on our wedding day," Claire said, playfully.

"I just had to see if my bride was going to meet me at the altar?"

"Why, of course," Claire chuckled. "I don't think I would miss this for the world!"

"Good, because I've got a surprise for you afterwards My Love." Henry teased her.

"Really? Now you've got my curiosity up!" Claire replied.

"You'll just have to wait and see," Henry said. "By the way, did you sleep well?"

"I sure did, but I woke up at 6:45. I must be a little excited, don't you think?"

"Well I know I am. It's been a long time since I've shared my life with someone. But I sure am looking forward to it!"

"Me too, Honey, and since it's almost 7:00, I better get some breakfast before the girls get here and start working on me!"

"Well, I don't think they will need to do much, Honey. But I will let you go. See you at 2:00pm sharp!"

"Yes, Darling, see you at the altar!" Smiling, Claire put the phone down, only to have it ring again. "Now Honey I told you—"

"Told me what?" Terry said, laughing.

"Oh, I'm sorry. I thought it was Henry calling back."

"I figured as much," Terry replied. "Just wanted to tell you that Martha and I will be over with the hairdresser around 10:30am and it shouldn't take more than a couple of hours to do your hair and makeup. Then we'll take the limo to the church around 12:45. That way we'll have a little time to take a few pictures before the ceremony starts."

"Wow, you've got everything planned out, don't you?"

"You kinda have too," Terry laughed.

"OK. Then I'm going to go eat a little breakfast before you get here, and finish packing my bags!"

"That would be great, because after the ceremony, you will want to just stop by, grab your bags and go on to the airport."

"Yes, Henry has that all worked out, thank goodness. Makes me tired just thinking about it!"

"Don't get stressed—relax and enjoy the day. It's going to be wonderful," Terry assured her.

"Thanks, Terry, for everything. I really do appreciate you and Martha helping out the way you have."

Unforeseen

"You're very welcome," Terry said, "and I'll see you soon!"

Claire was on the way to the kitchen when her phone rang again. "My goodness, it's sure getting busy around here," she said, as she picked up the receiver. "Hello?"

"Claire? This is Marisa. Hope I'm not bothering you?"

"Not at all," Claire said. "So glad you called. So, how are you?"

"I'm doing well. I just wanted to say that I'm so sorry I couldn't be a bridesmaid. I was just afraid to wear heels just yet."

"That's all right, Dear. How is your ankle doing?"

"Oh, it's getting better every day. I'm able to walk pretty good now—just not doing anything like fancy dancing," she laughed. "I'm going to try to come to the service. What time did you say it was?"

"It's at 2:00pm Honey. And we will have a row reserved for family, near the front."

"Is it OK if I bring my fiancé?"

"Of course, he's more than welcome to come!"

"Great, I will see you there!"

Claire put the phone down and finally made herself a pot of coffee and some toast. As she prayed, she thanked the Lord for putting so many wonderful people in her life, and thanked Mr. Peterson for his generosity and vision for giving others a second chance at life.

The church was full, and the ushers were busy deciding which side to put people on. "Never seen this many people at a second-time wedding," one usher chuckled.

"I know," Martha commented, hurriedly instructing those in the bridal party and folding more bulletins, it seemed they were going to run low.

"I didn't know Claire'd invited so many people," Terry remarked.

"Well, perhaps it's people from all the other inheritance meetings," Martha grinned.

"I think it's great," Trent said, as he was trying to fix his tie.

"Come here," said Martha, jerking him around and inspecting him from head to toe. "Let me help you with that," she laughed.

"Hey, thanks. I thought I was going to choke!"

Suddenly, Tom ran in the door a little out of breath, "I just got in from picking up some people at the airport, thought we were going to be late!" When Tom noticed Terry, he couldn't say anything for a minute.

"Is everything OK?" Martha said, "Is your tie too tight, as well?" she grinned.

"What?" Tom said, fumbling. "Uh, no, I'm fine. I don't believe we've met?" He held out his hand to shake Terry's.

"Hi, I'm Terry Morgan, and you are?"

"I'm Henry's son, Tom Anderson."

"Oh, we love your dad. He's the most wonderful man!"

"Well, I'm glad you approve. I'd like to think I come from that same wonderful stock," he grinned.

Blushing, she laughed, "Yes, I'm sure you do!"

"So, you are a bridesmaid?" Tom asked.

"As a matter of fact, I am."

"Well, perhaps I'll be the one escorting you down the aisle?" Tom wondered. Martha quickly scanned the sheet of paper with all the instructions.

"Why, yes, Tom. It seems you will be," she grinned first at him, then Terry.

Unforeseen

Looking outside, Tom saw Marisa coming down the sidewalk with her fiancé. *Oh, thank the Lord,* he said to himself. When she came in, they hugged, and he proceeded to escort them down to the row reserved for family. Whispering in her ear, he said, "So glad you all came for Dad!"

"I am too," Marisa smiled. "I'm really happy for him."

As they sat down, she noticed all the people there. Thinking back at the call she had made to her dad last week, she knew she had surprised him with her gift of a week at her chateau in France. *Well, it's the least I could do* she thought, *with all he did for me while I was off my feet.* She remembered his early morning calls, cards, and all the visits he had made as she was recuperating.

Henry seemed as cool as a cucumber. Walking into the foyer, he looked around grinning. "Well is everyone ready?"

Martha spoke saying, "Yes, I believe it's almost time!"

"Where is my bride?"

"She's waiting right inside that door, "Terry grinned. "And it's not good luck to see her before the wedding either."

"Well I don't believe in luck, do you?" Everyone looked at Martha who seemed a little surprised.

"No, I guess not," she responded slowly.

"Then would you mind escorting me over there?" he smiled.

"Why, ah, sure," she said, and took his arm. As she opened the door, his mouth dropped open when he saw Claire.

"Oh my. What a vision of beauty you are My Dear!"

Smiling, she looked down, embarrassed. "Well, I wanted to be as beautiful as I could be for you," she said softy.

"You are," Henry reached down and kissed her on the cheek. Whispering in her ear, "Just wanted to tell you that I can't wait to be your husband." Then he shut the door and noticed that everyone was looking his way, wiping their eyes.

"Shall we proceed?" he asked, smiling, and with that the service began.

Chapter 48

The ceremony was breath taking, not glitzy or glamorous, but a sweetness prevailed that was evident to all. Guests mingled in the church, and no one wanted to leave.

Terry looked up to see Tom watching her from across the sanctuary. Suddenly, becoming shy, she looked away.

Stressed, Martha came up to Terry and asked "Can you help me with getting the people to move towards their cars. We need to get the reception started. We only have the room for two hours!"

"Sure," Terry said and quickly forgot about Tom as she began to tell people where the reception would be. She looked up and saw Tom by her side.

"So," he said smiling, "looks like we are the last ones to leave. Would you like to ride over with me and the girls?"

"Well, sure," Terry said a little off guard, "I suppose that would be fine, although my car is here at the church."

"That's OK, I won't leave you stranded. I promise I will bring you back afterwards."

"Why not?" she smiled and grabbed her purse on the way out.

As people gathered at the reception, Clay and Matthew mingled around the tables nibbling on all the desserts. Sandy joined them carrying little Emma. "Oh, my what a beautiful child!" Melissa said, reaching out to touch the little girl. "She looks just like you two!

"Thanks!" Matthew grinned. "But I think she's got more of her mom's good looks!" Sandy laughed, and handed the little girl to Melissa.

"So, how you two been doing?" asked Matthew.

"Who us?" Clay laughed and looked over at Melissa who rolled her eyes. "We are doing great! I'm having the time of my life being married, aren't you, Honey?"

"Yes, who would've known that night in the hospital, when I was dead tired after a twelve-hour shift, I would be meeting my husband!"

Sandy spoke up and said, "Well, that's the way I felt when I first met Matthew. I thought 'Who is this handsome guy coming all the way over to the Sudan, out of the blue?' It only took me a few weeks to realize that I was falling in love with him."

"Really?" Matthew winked, "I thought I had you at 'Hello!'" With that they laughed so loud everyone looked over at them.

"We better pipe down a little," Clay grinned. "Everyone will think we've had something stronger to drink!"

Just then Nicole came over and hugged little Emma! "You all are having way too much fun!"

"We're just catching up. It's been way too long!" Clay replied.

"I know, and I feel so bad about that. Here we are in the same city, and we don't stay in touch like we promised we would do," Nicole said frowning.

"We weren't any better. So, don't take all the blame," Clay remarked.

Unforeseen

"Yeah," Matthew said, "We should do a better job of communicating more often" he frowned.

"Don't beat yourself up," Nicole shook her head, "life happens. However, now that we are reunited, perhaps we can all do better in the future!"

"Sounds good to us!" Sandy smiled.

"So, how are you doing, Nicole?" Sandy asked. "How are the shelters running? I've heard you opened several more of them?"

"Yes, we've opened two more, and they are really a blessing! I've got my hands full, but I've got good assistants, who do most of the work. Especially now that I'm having to take some time off from work."

"What's wrong?" Melissa asked.

"Well, they've found more cancer. I'd been cancer free for over a year. Then I started having some headaches, and I went to the doctor. They saw some tumors in my brain."

Melissa looked at Clay who glanced towards Matthew and Sandy.

"Oh, no, Nicole. We're so sorry to hear that! Is there anything we can do?" Melissa asked. "I know some great cancer doctors."

But before she could finish, Nicole stopped her and said, "Listen everyone, the Lord has healed me before, and I believe He will again. I don't think my time is over yet, although I know none of us wants to die. I believe that I still have more to do before that time comes, and I know that is going to work out in my favor!"

"Wow, that's a great outlook!" Clay said.

"It sure is!" Matthew smiled. "We will all keep you in our prayers!"

"Thank you, that means the world to me," and as she turned around, Rob was right there behind her.

"We sure do appreciate your prayers," Rob said, "It's hard to see her go through chemo again, but God will see us through." he smiled.

As they nodded in agreement, they heard the piano playing, and the M.C. announcing the arrival of the bride and groom. Claire came into the room smiling and waving to the different people she knew. Then her eyes fell on Clay, and the group! "Henry, I've got to go over and speak to my friends."

"Sure, Honey, I would love to meet them too." Soon everyone was hugging and talking at the same time.

"Claire, you look so radiant!" Nicole said, smiling.

"Yes, you look very happy," Matthew said, as he tried to get Emma to take her bottle.

"Oh, look at that bundle of joy! Matthew, can you believe in just two years how your life has changed?" Claire smiled.

"No, I still have to pinch myself!" he grinned.

"And Clay, your wife is just beautiful! Henry, please meet Clay, and Melissa."

Henry shook everyone's hand and said, "So nice meeting all of you! Tom has told me all about you."

"How do you know Tom?" Nicole asked.

"Oh, he's my son!" Henry grinned broadly.

"Really? Katie, his wife and I were very close friends. In fact, when she passed away, I stepped in to assist with her ministry."

"Oh, I've heard what a wonderful lady she was. I wish I had gotten to meet her. Unfortunately, Tom and I just reconnected after many years. It's a long story, I don't want to bore you with here."

Claire made her way over and pulled Nicole off to the side. "So how are you feeling, Nicole?" You look beautiful!"

"Why, thank you. The Lord has been good, and I really believe that He will heal me again."

"That's wonderful. If you should need anything, don't hesitant to give me a call, anytime!"

Unforeseen

"Thank you, Claire. You've been so kind to all of us!"

"Well, I guess we better get to the front, Honey. I hear our names being called," and Henry ushered Claire towards the cake.

"Doesn't she look radiant?" Sandy said, smiling. "Reminds me of our wedding, Honey!"

"Yes, it's all such a blur, isn't it?" Melissa said, and they all chuckled.

As the dancing got underway, Tom noticed Terry and Martha near the door chatting with Clay and the group. Strolling over, everyone looked up, and Nicole was the first to run over and grab him, hugging him tightly. "Tom, it's so good to see you!"

"Nicole, how are you doing? I should have called!"

"I'm fine, don't worry. How are the girls?"

"Oh, they're great, adjusting nicely—and even giving their ole dad a run for his money!"

As Clay and Matthew spoke to him, Tom kept noticing Terry and the easy way she smiled and carried herself. Just as Tom started to walk toward her, suddenly the door opened, and a man came through pushing a wheelchair with a young woman in it.

Claire and Henry both looked up, and Terry and Martha went running over and started hugging them. "Who's that?" Tom spoke up.

"I'm not sure?" Matthew and Clay both replied, "but it must be someone from the second group."

As Terry gained her composure, she walked over to Clay, and the others and explained who Maggie was, and what had happened to cause her to be in a wheelchair.

"How wonderful that they could be here too!" Nicole smiled.

As the music started again, she grabbed Rob's hand and said, "Honey, let's dance!"

Looking over Terry's way, Tom said quietly, "Would you like to dance?"

"Sure, that would be nice," she smiled. And soon everyone was on the dance floor.

Martha stood there, watching everyone laughing and having a good time. Suddenly a man's voice behind her asked if she would like to dance. Looking up, she noticed a handsome older gentleman smiling.

"Why not?" she smiled, "It is time to celebrate isn't it?"

"Yes, I would say so" he replied, and took her hand in his.

THE END

Unforeseen

Victoria Lynn Deviney

ACKNOWLEDGEMENT

First of all, I want to give God all the glory for allowing me the opportunity to write. This was one of those "bucket list" items I had prayed about one day that I never thought I would have the time or ability to do.

Secondly, I want to thank my husband who gave me the encouragement and pushed me to complete this sequel!

Lastly, a big shout out to my editor Phyllis Dolislager for staying on me to publish and get this book out.

Without my God, my family, and my friends, I would not see the fulfillment of a dream I've had for a long time—for that I am so grateful.

Made in the USA
Columbia, SC
08 September 2018